South Shore Billionaires

Billionaires finding brides!

Bonded at boarding school, best friends Jeremy, Branson and Cole have scaled the world's rich lists and become New York's wealthiest tycoons.

Now these billionaires are swapping the bright lights of the city for the blue waters and golden sands of the coast. In stunning South Shore, they'll find love and taste a life they never knew they wanted!

Read Jeremy's story in
Christmas Baby for the Billionaire

Discover Branson's story in
Beauty and the Brooding Billionaire

And find out Cole's story in
The Billionaire's Island Bride

All available now!

Dear Reader,

There are times when bits of my real life trickle into my books. That's certainly the case with *The Billionaire's Island Bride*! As I was writing this one, a hurricane came up the east coast and Nova Scotia got a direct hit. Our power was out for nearly three days—thank goodness for our generator! In that time, I did a lot of reading by either lantern light or the one lamp we plugged in. The generator doesn't run the whole house, but it kept our fridge and freezer running. Food, wine and a good book—what more does one need, really?

The other element in this book that touches home for me is Marvin, the dog. We lost our beloved Dreamer, a Nova Scotia Duck Tolling Retriever, in 2018. But there is something so perfectly joyous about a rousing game of fetch, or petting soft and silky ears, or just knowing a dog is there next to you when you're having a rough day. We're thinking it might almost be time to add another pup to our family...but we're unsure of how the cats are going to feel about it, of course!

I hope you enjoy this final story in the South Shore Billionaires trilogy.

Happy reading,

Donna

The Billionaire's Island Bride

Donna Alward

HARLEQUIN®
® *Romance*™

Recycling programs
for this product may
not exist in your area.

ISBN-13: 978-1-335-55631-8

The Billionaire's Island Bride

This edition published by arrangement with Harlequin Books S.A.

For questions and comments about the quality of this book,
please contact us at CustomerService@Harlequin.com.

Harlequin Enterprises ULC
22 Adelaide St. West, 40th Floor
Toronto, Ontario M5H 4E3, Canada
www.Harlequin.com

Printed in U.S.A.

Donna Alward lives on Canada's east coast.
Her heartwarming stories of love, hope and
homecoming have been translated into several
languages, hit bestseller lists and won awards,
but her favorite thing is hearing from readers!
When she's not writing she enjoys reading (of
course), knitting, gardening, cooking...and she is a
Masterpiece Theatre addict. You can visit her on
the web at donnaalward.com and join her mailing
list at donnaalward.com/newsletter.

Books by Donna Alward

Harlequin Romance

South Shore Billionaires

Christmas Baby for the Billionaire
Beauty and the Brooding Billionaire

Destination Brides

Summer Escape with the Tycoon

Marrying a Millionaire

Best Man for the Wedding Planner
Secret Millionaire for the Surrogate

Heart to Heart

Hired: The Italian's Bride

How a Cowboy Stole Her Heart

Visit the Author Profile page
at Harlequin.com for more titles.

To Dreamer, the best dog

Praise for
Donna Alward

"Ms. Alward wrote a wonderfully emotional story
that is not to be missed. She provided a tale
rich with emotions, filled with sexual chemistry,
wonderful dialogue, and endearing characters....
I highly recommend *Summer Escape with the
Tycoon* to other readers."

—*Goodreads*

CHAPTER ONE

BROOKLYN GRAVES HEARD the *whomp-whomp-whomp* of helicopter rotors and rolled her eyes, then let out a long breath as she turned her back on the cliff and followed its progress.

The wind off the ocean whipped her hair around her face and she shoved it back with a hand, tucking it behind her ears, where it stayed for all of about ten seconds before it was loose and blowing around again. She shaded her eyes and stared at the red-and-white chopper as it arced over her corner of the island and then headed toward the grand house and the helipad there.

She'd known this day was coming. Ernest Chetwynd had finally sold the island, and an American had bought it. If the ostentatious aerial arrival was anything to go by, Cole Abbott was going to be a real piece of work. Money to throw around on private islands, and an ego to match.

The sound faded, muffled by the rhythmic roar of the waves crashing on the rocks below. Ernest, who had been the one to build the landing pad, had occasionally had a helicopter chartered. He'd taken her up once, on her birthday, and given her a tour of the Nova Scotia south shore. It had been so different seeing it from the air, all the rugged rocks and islands and sandy beaches. And utterly harmless, since Ernest had been at least seventy-five at that time. He was lonely, and she and Ernest had been friends of a sort. There'd certainly been mutual respect, making her presence on the island quite secure.

His big mansion had once housed him and his wife, and then quite often their children and grandchildren. After Marietta's death, everything had changed. Ernest went to see his kids instead. The house—all twelve thousand square feet of it—was too much for an aging bachelor, even though he'd hired Brooklyn to care for the grounds and he had a housekeeper come over from the mainland once a week.

As long as Ernest had owned the island, Brooklyn had been safe. She owned the southeast corner, a wonderful acreage passed down by her great-grandparents, and which provided her with solitude and peace and an amazing atmosphere to make a living. Her little boat ensured that she could get back and forth to the mainland whenever she wanted. And she did, often. For supplies and visits with friends. But always, Bellwether Island had been there for her to retreat to. Her safe haven.

Which was now spoiled by the new owner, who was ostentatiously arriving by chopper, now that crews had ferried his things from the mainland to the island and delivered them to the grand house on the bluff. She'd started calling him Mr. Fancy Man in her head.

In short, she was not happy about this new development, even though she'd known it was bound to happen. Ernest couldn't hold on forever, and she'd hoped one of his kids would take it over. But none of them wanted it—not the isolation of being the only occupants of the island, nor the upkeep. Just some American billionaire who wanted to add it to his list of...well, whatever. Accomplishments? Possessions? It didn't matter.

She let out another breath and started the walk back to the house. The sound of the waves faded, though the wind still tossed her hair around. She stopped at the vegetable garden behind the century-old house. The garden was nearly done now, in mid-September. It had been a good summer, a little dry, perhaps, but with enough rain to fill Brooklyn's water tanks for when Mother Nature needed a little help. She'd spent every summer here as a kid, running over the island, swimming on the beach and helping her grandmother with gardening and canning while her grandfather fished. There'd been a hammock between two spruce trees, and she'd spent hours there curled up with a book. Almost every good memory she had of her childhood was tied to this island. It was why, when everything in her life fell horrifically apart, she'd come back. To the place where she'd last felt safe and happy. And here she'd stayed.

Now that peaceful existence was threatened. Because exactly one week ago, on the day that Cole Abbott took possession of Bellwether Island, she'd received an offer from his attorney, attempting to buy her out.

One she'd rejected immediately. The truth was, despite the gorgeous mansion and spectacular setting, living here wasn't always easy. Popping to the store for a last-minute item couldn't happen. Going out to dinner took planning, taking the weather and tides into account. And in the winter, it was downright isolating. She'd bet a hundred bucks that Abbott would be gone once he'd sat through his first January northeaster. And then she wouldn't have to worry about him, except for maybe a few months of the year. The shine would certainly wear off his new toy.

She just had to do what she always did: persevere.

Cole hopped out of the helicopter and reached back for his duffel bag. With a wave to the pilot, he ran from the helipad toward the house. He was nearly to the back garden when the chopper lifted off again and started back toward mainland Nova Scotia.

He was finally here.

In a few days, work crews would ferry over and begin the renovations he had planned, and in early October, his first corporate retreat was booked, from one of his own companies. The executives were scheduled to stay four days, for rest, rejuvenation and an informal sharing of ideas while they unplugged.

During this event, there would be no Wi-Fi provided. His team would enjoy top-notch dining, an on-site gym, the hot tub, and the sound of the ocean. An antidote to the high-pressure lives they led and a way to keep them from burning out and to remind them of why they loved their careers.

He wished he'd had such a thing not so long ago.

The keys to his house were in his pocket, but

he put his bag by the door and then ventured down to the beach. It wasn't large—maybe two hundred feet of sandy shoreline that gave way to rocks, but it was enough. The September day was warm, and he took off his shoes and socks and rolled up the cuffs of his jeans, letting his toes squidge in the sand. Wind blew the short strands of his hair off his face, and he drew the salt air into his lungs. Ten extra steps led him to the water, where the cold Atlantic fizzed over his toes. The breakers washed over his ankles, splashing a little and dampening his jeans. But he didn't care.

Having his Realtor best friend, Jeremy, find this place was the answer to a prayer.

Cole let out a breath and pulled in another. And another. A year ago he'd found himself on a dangerous path. One that mimicked his father's, including a cardiac episode that had scared him to death. He didn't want to end like his dad, dead at fifty-one—or thirty-five—from a heart attack because he'd been a workaholic.

Work hard, play hard. That was what Jeremy and Bran had always said about him. He never did anything halfway. Maybe not. He did tend to commit fully to something when he took it on. But in this case, it wasn't about achieving. It was about living.

He dawdled in the water for nearly an hour, before heading back to the house and finally going inside.

It was a cavernous edifice for one person: twelve thousand square feet of understated luxury. There was a not-too-big garage, but it was enough to house a golf cart for getting around the island, and maintenance machinery, like the small tractor for mowing the grass and various garden implements. And a snow blower. He shivered, thinking about how bleak it would be here in the middle of a winter storm. And yet…there was something comforting about being snug inside while the outside was wild and untamed. He certainly couldn't live here year round. He still had responsibilities. At thirty-five, retirement wasn't an option. He still ran his father's empire of manufacturing companies, and he needed that challenge. But he was less hands-on than he used to be, delegating far more responsibility. His hope was to spend maybe a third of the year here, overseeing the corporate retreat business, and two thirds back in Manhattan, home of the headquarters of Abbott Industries.

His things were already in the room he'd chosen for himself, a large suite facing southeast, with windows overlooking the beach and down the island, where the roof of the farmhouse was just visible among the trees. He put down his duffel and went to the window. Brooklyn Graves. That was the name of the woman who lived there, the one who refused to sell her parcel of land. It complicated things, in his mind. They shared access to the dock, which wasn't really sufficient to his needs, and she owned the boathouse at the tip of the island. He'd hired a husband and wife to be caretakers here, and right now they had to be housed in the apartment above the garage. It would be far better if they could live in the farmhouse and have their own real home.

If only stubborn Ms. Graves would sell. What on earth was a single woman doing living on an island twelve months of the year, anyway?

He knew little about her, except that she ran some sort of cottage industry—had Jeremy mentioned knitting or something?—from her home and that her family had lived on the island for generations. He would have to put on the charm and visit, make her come around. She sounded like the type to offer him tea and scones. Knitting? She was probably someone's reclusive aunt, too stubborn to move. It might take all his powers of persuasion.

He didn't really want to, but he figured he should introduce himself as soon as possible.

The longer he put it off, the more awkward it was bound to become. Chances were his reception would be chilly, anyway.

With a last look out the window, he turned away and went back downstairs, and out the front door this time. He'd just walk down to meet her and break the ice. He wouldn't even mention selling. Not yet.

The front gardens were beautiful. The grass was neatly trimmed, and there were still flowers, yellow and red and rusty-colored ones, brightening the beds. Further along, past the manicured lawns, the landscape was wilder. One either side of the lane was waving grass and thick bunches of goldenrod and light purple wild asters. Most of the trees were evergreens, with very little hardwood, but here and there he saw birches and maples. The leaves on the birches were starting to yellow, but the maples were still green and vibrant. The walk took maybe only ten, fifteen minutes, tops, but it was a beautiful one.

The farmhouse came into view and he stopped for a moment, struck by the sight of it. It was old and rambling, but well kept, with freshly painted spindles on the veranda and potted flowers on the stained steps. There was nothing special about it really; the outside was white, with no fancy trim or shutters, but it was charming and cozy and like something he expected to see on an old-time greeting card. All that was missing was—

A bark sounded and a retriever bounded from around the corner of the house, straight toward him. Apparently a dog *wasn't* missing from the picture, and he resisted the urge to roll his eyes at the homey scene. Eyes bright and tongue lolling happily, the dog ran up to him and immediately rubbed against his legs, looking for pats.

Cole couldn't help obliging. He loved dogs. Not that he'd ever had one growing up.

"Who's a good boy?" He rubbed the dog's head and then laughed when the dog dropped to the grass and rolled over, showing his belly. Cole willingly knelt down and gave him a belly rub, chuckling at the obvious enjoyment of the pooch as he rolled his back this way and that, legs in the air. Dogs were just so pure in everything they did. No agendas. Unlike himself...

"Marvin, come."

The female voice jolted him from his thoughts and he stood, leaving Marvin on his back with his paws up. A clap from the owner of the voice had the dog jumping up and shaking all over, then trotting back to his human's side.

Cole's brain momentarily emptied. All the

opening lines he'd imagined flew straight out of his head and away on the ocean breeze. He'd expected someone middle-aged or older. A... spinster. Not a thirtyish woman with hair the color of peanut butter, wearing skinny jeans, boots, and a sweater that nipped in at her waist and hugged her hips.

This was Brooklyn Graves?

"You're Mr. Abbott."

He realized he'd been standing there for long seconds and saying absolutely nothing. He nodded, then moved forward and held out his hand. "Yes, Cole Abbott. It's good to finally meet."

More than good. Wow.

She didn't smile as she shook his hand. As he got closer he noticed that a few freckles dotted her nose, and her eyes were a clear, clear blue. Her hand was warm and strong, and he felt a few rough spots at the base of her fingers. Calluses? Interesting.

She dropped his hand and stepped back. "What can I do for you, Mr. Abbott?"

"Please, call me Cole." He tried a warm smile, but it didn't appear to be getting him anywhere. "We're neighbors, after all."

She gave a shrug with one shoulder. "Well, I know you'd like to change that, so I'll be as clear as I can. I'm not interested in selling my house or acreage."

Cole took a few moments to gather himself before responding. In the end, he tried a small smile. "I got your reply, Ms. Graves. I truly did just come down to say hello. The island will be pretty small if we aren't on speaking terms."

"Tell me you don't want to buy me out and we can be the best of friends." She put her hands on her hips, and Marvin the dog sat at her feet, the soul of loyalty and obedience.

He couldn't lie to her. For one, he got the sneaky suspicion she'd see right through it. For another, lying always came back to bite him in the butt.

Instead he put away his "let's be friends" face, choosing instead a more businesslike manner. "I'll be honest. I would like to buy your property." He figured it wouldn't hurt to sweeten the pot. "What I'm prepared to offer can set you up somewhere very nicely."

His initial offer had been for three hundred and fifty thousand dollars. The house would likely need renovations and the dock definitely needed work. It had been…reasonable.

"Would you pay me a million dollars?"

Her gaze was sharp and pinned him in place, but he'd been in business a long time. He knew how to hide his reactions, and right now he wanted to chuckle a little bit. He'd paid seven million for the rest of the land and house and considered it a steal. Her property accounted for maybe, at best, a sixth of the island. A million wasn't that outrageous, really. Not considering the buildings on the property and the dock access.

"Yes." Heck, if all it took was a million bucks to get her to sign away the deed, he'd do it happily. Jeremy had been the one to recommend lowballing. Cole didn't mind upping the ante. "Yes, I'm prepared to offer you a million."

She started at him a long moment and then turned away. "I don't think so," she said and started walking toward the house. "Come, Marvin."

The dog jumped up and trotted at her heels. Meanwhile, Cole stood flummoxed on her front path, staring at her as she went in through the screen door, took Marvin with her and let the door fall shut with a loud snap behind them.

Huh. So, round one and two to Ms. Graves. But Cole wasn't done yet. He had a history of getting what he wanted, and this was nothing more than a challenge.

CHAPTER TWO

BROOKLYN SAT IN her favorite chair, yarn trailing perfectly from her yarn bowl to the needles, and adjusted the weight of the shawl she was knitting. It was a simple pattern but incredibly lovely, both stylish and warm, and this was one item she was knitting for herself and not to sell.

The click of the needles in the silence gave her comfort, which was good. She'd come inside yesterday after talking to Cole Abbott and had shaken for a good thirty minutes. Confrontation was not her thing. She knew how to be strong but it had cost her, stealing her energy, prompting a near panic attack.

Marvin had stayed close all evening, soothing her and being steady and reliable with his company. At one point her therapist had asked if she wanted to get a service dog, but Brooklyn had declined. She had Marvin. And she'd come a very long way since she'd started counseling. She'd come to the island to escape and heal, but she'd stayed because she'd built a life she truly loved. And if she was occasionally lonely…oh, well. She'd learned that there were worse things in life than loneliness. She had everything just the way she wanted it here. No surprises.

Her needles slowed. Still, she'd coexisted with Ernest and his extended family without any trouble, and she'd admit—only to herself— that just knowing someone else was on the island had been a comfort. She wasn't sure she could say the same about Cole Abbott. His very presence threatened the life she'd built for herself.

Maybe she should head over to the mainland tomorrow and get out for a bit. Pick up a few groceries, perhaps go for a coffee with Delilah or Jen, the sisters who ran the yarn and craft store in Liverpool. Hadn't she just told herself that she needed to be patient? Mr. Fancy Man wouldn't be on the island forever. It would be another plaything he'd tire of and move on. But her life…it would remain unchanged. Just the way she wanted it.

The morning dawned foggy, but by ten it had burned off and the mellow September sun had warmed the air. Brooklyn carried a large handbag over her shoulder, which contained fabric shopping bags, her wallet, her phone, and a leash for Marvin, who always joined her on her trips to town. In her hands were five small shipping boxes containing orders ready to be shipped to customers of her online store. She turned the corner toward the dock and stopped short. There was a second boat anchored there, and Cole stood on the dock while another man moved around, taking pictures with his phone.

What the heck were they doing? It wasn't as if Cole didn't have a reason to be there. He did. Their access to the dock was shared.

The sight of him, though, was unexpected. And she couldn't deny that she rather enjoyed seeing him in faded jeans and a dark blue windbreaker. He looked…normal. Not like some rich tycoon, which he most certainly must be.

He caught sight of her and smiled, then waved. "Ms. Graves. Good morning."

"Good morning," she replied and wished she'd put Marvin on his leash, because at the friendly sound of Cole's voice, the dog trotted off for more pats and head rubs.

Traitor.

"Marvin, come," she called. But Marvin was too busy having his ears rubbed to pay much attention. Brooklyn sighed and went toward the two men, both to get Marvin and to satisfy her curiosity about what was going on.

"I'd say you're spoiling him, but I'm not sure it's possible to spoil a dog with pats," she said, trying to be friendly. Things had been tense during their earlier conversation. Establishing a little peace didn't mean she'd changed her mind.

"He's hard to resist. What a friendly guy." Cole's tone left a hint of insinuation, perhaps that her dog was more amiable than she was. Which was true.

"Is there a problem or something?" She stared pointedly at the other man, who was now at the end of the dock, writing something on a clipboard.

"Oh, Mike. Hey, Mike, come meet Brooklyn Graves. We share docking privileges."

Mike came over and held out his hand. "Nice to meet you, Brooklyn."

Cole turned to her. "Mike's going to make some repairs and mods to the dock. It doesn't quite suit my needs."

Her heart stuttered. Sure, the dock was old but it was sturdy and sound. She adjusted her packages and briefly shook Mike's hand. "What sort of needs?"

Cole answered. "Your boat's small, but I need to be able to accommodate bigger vessels.

I've hired Mike to expand it and also make any repairs necessary."

She wanted to be angry, and she would be later, but right now all she felt was shock and amazement at his audacity. "Um, you do remember that we share the dock, right?"

He bestowed another one of those charming smiles on her. "Well, of course. I'm sure Mike will have no trouble splitting the invoice between us."

Another layer of shock rippled through her. Share the cost? How was she supposed to pay for that? A hole opened up in her middle, the place where worry and panic seemed to live. The hole was soon filled with indignation.

"You can't do that without consulting me first."

At her sharp tone, Marvin moved away from Cole and went to sit at her heel. Mike discreetly left the conversation and continued on with his assessment.

"Oh. Well, I could just foot the bill, if…"

Her mouth tightened as she finally let the anger in. "If I sell to you, right? That's what this is all about? I won't sell so you're going to bankrupt me with foolish repairs?" She mentally calculated her equity between the house, business and her savings account, and lifted her chin. "Do I need to consult my lawyer on this, Mr. Abbott?"

She was reasonably sure that he couldn't just do repairs without getting her to sign off on them. But he'd make sure she spent legal fees to guarantee it, wouldn't he? Fire burned in her veins. Why did successful, rich people always have to get their own way and swing their power around like a mace?

"Now, Ms. Graves…"

She stepped back. "Don't you dare *Ms. Graves* me, especially in that patronizing tone. At this rate, *Mister* Abbott…" she paused and let the emphasis on the word ring in the air. "…I would not sell to you for a million dollars. Or two million. My great-grandparents were the first people to live on this island. My great-grandfather was a fisherman, like his father before him. My grandparents lived here and brought up five children. I spent every summer as a kid here and I know each square foot of it better in my sleep than you ever will. Maybe our family doesn't own the entire island anymore, but my corner of it is still mine. And I am not for sale."

Her hands were shaking, so she clutched the boxes tighter as she stared at him.

"Noted," he said quietly.

"Now, if you will excuse me, I am going to

get on *my* boat and pilot it to the mainland. Marvin, come."

This time Marvin obeyed immediately, falling in at her heel without need of a leash or a second urging.

She made it to the boat with sure steps, got them both aboard and stowed her bag and parcels. It wasn't until she'd untied from the dock and steered away that she relaxed her shoulders and tried to suck in big, calming gulps of air.

She was okay. This was not the same as… that other time. He did not have a weapon and she was not in danger. Her body response had been triggered but she worked her way through the reaction until she wasn't shaking any longer. She looked over her shoulder and couldn't see the dock anymore, or Cole and Mike. It was almost as if it had never happened.

No, Cole Abbott hadn't threatened her person. Instead, he had threatened her security and the life she'd built for herself. Maybe it wasn't as frightening as an assault on a visceral level, but the idea of change was terrifying to her.

How many times was someone supposed to start over? Maybe in the past she'd given up too easily. Well, not this time. This time she would fight tooth and nail to preserve what was important to her. And if that meant dipping into her very small savings account for a visit to the lawyer, then that was what she'd do.

Cole had messed up again. He'd planned on the conversation with Brooklyn going differently. The idea had been for him to do the dock repairs as a gesture of goodwill. But he'd teased, and she'd taken him seriously, bringing legal advice into it. He'd miscalculated.

Now he too was on the mainland, sitting in his best friend, Jeremy Fisher's rather large kitchen, drinking coffee and feeling grouchy about it all. His other pal, Branson Black, was back in New York, dealing with getting his brownstone ready to sell. While Jeremy was settled with his new wife and baby, Branson's love life was up in the air since the departure of artist Jessica Blundon, who had spent the summer on the south shore.

Cole's love life was nonexistent, and he was okay with that. For now, anyway. He had too much going on to devote much time to a relationship. Even a casual one. And he wasn't sure he was capable of any other kind. It wasn't like he'd had a stellar example growing up.

"So she threatened to go to her lawyer?" Jeremy reentered the kitchen, his baby daughter on his arm. She'd just awakened from a nap, and Jeremy's wife, Tori, was running errands.

It was still an adjustment, seeing his friend so settled into domestic life.

"I know. I meant to tell her that I would cover the cost since I was the one needing the modifications, but she got the jump on me and I took the bait. She's very prickly about the fact I made her an offer." He took a sip of his coffee. "This morning she told me she wouldn't sell for two million dollars."

Jeremy laughed. "Well, it's her home. And clearly she's attached to it. What's the big deal, anyway? It's not like there isn't enough room for the two of you. You're not even going to be there all year round."

Cole thought about it. "I'll be honest. Some of it is ego. I mean, I don't like being told no and I look at it as an extra challenge to get my way."

Jeremy met his gaze, his eyes alight with humor. "How very self-aware of you. But gee, Cole, you were never competitive in school."

"I see you haven't lost your talent for sarcasm," Cole answered. "And hey, I know that trait can be a strength or a weakness, depending on the situation. She's not what I expected."

"How so?"

"You said she ran some sort of business from her home, knitting or some such. I was expecting someone…hell, someone not young and pretty and…"

His voice trailed off. The truth was, as infuriating as their two conversations had been, he had found them invigorating.

Jeremy's laughter drew him back to the moment. He held Rose in one arm as he prepped a bottle with his free hand. "So she's pretty."

Cole sighed. "To be honest? Stunning. Beautiful hair, big eyes, nice body. But it's more than that. She's a strong woman, Jer. She's got to be, to live out there by herself. It's not far offshore but it's cut off from everything, especially in bad weather. She hopped on that boat today and steered away the way we'd get in a car and drive to the store."

"Ah. A woman who is capable and doesn't need rescuing. Interesting."

"Shut up." He took a long drink of coffee and grinned behind the rim. A bit of ribbing from his best friend made the world seem all right after all.

Rose was grumbling, so Jeremy tested the bottle and then began to feed her, standing right there in the kitchen. Cole was not good with babies. Not even a little. But even he had to admit that Rose was cute. There'd been a recent health scare as she'd contracted measles, but she seemed completely recovered now.

"So what's your game plan now?" Jeremy

asked, perching on a bar stool across the counter from Cole.

"I don't know. She'd see right through flowers or some sort of gift. Maybe I should just apologize and do a better job of explaining."

Jeremy looked at him for a long moment. "Cake. Take her cake. Or a bottle of wine or something. Just don't go empty-handed. And yeah, maybe explain that you got off on the wrong foot."

Cole considered for a minute. "Good suggestions. Or at least half of a good suggestion. I have an idea for the other."

"You sure you're not interested in her?" Jeremy asked, removing the bottle and wiping Rose's chin before giving her the bottle again. "When was the last time you went on a date?"

Cole's smile slipped away. The last time had been over a year ago, just before his world had come crashing down.

Not that anyone really knew anything about that. He'd been able to hide it really well. Faking his way through stuff was his specialty. Even Bran and Jeremy didn't know the true extent of what had happened.

"It's been a long time. But no, that would just get messy, wouldn't it? Besides, as you say, I'm only planning to be here part of the year. I do still have Abbott to run."

And that required him to be in New York. Not on an island in the Atlantic off the coast of Nova Scotia. The island was to be his retreat. And hopefully he could offer the same to his own executives.

The hum of the garage door opener interrupted the silence. "Tori's home. Are you staying for dinner?"

Cole looked at his watch and then shook his head. "Naw, but thanks. I have those errands to run and then pick up the boat. I'm leaving the car at the marina garage." He looked up as Tori came inside, a bag of produce in her hands. "Hello, gorgeous."

"Hey, Cole. How are things on the island?"

Jeremy jumped in. "The farmhouse owner is a hottie."

"Of course she is. Brooklyn has a really neat business, too. She runs an online store and ships all over. Knitted items but she also dyes her own yarn and sells it. And her big thing is patterns. She develops patterns and sells them. One was even picked up by some big magazine last year. She's wicked smart. Her overhead is really low and she doesn't have a mortgage since she inherited the house from her grandparents."

Cole stared at her. "You knew?"

Tori laughed and started taking vegetables

out of the bag. "Of course I knew. This is a small town and I've lived in the area my whole life."

"You didn't say anything in the summer, when we went over there."

"Why should I? You were buying the rest of the land, not hers." Her brows pulled together in confusion. "Why? What happened?"

Jeremy put the bottle down and put Rose up on his shoulder as he patted her back. "Cole offered to buy her out, and made her pretty angry from the sounds of it. She threatened to lawyer up."

Tori nodded. "Good for her. That place means a lot to her."

"It does?"

Tori seemed to hesitate, her hand resting on a large bundle of leeks. "It's been in her family a long time," she finally said. "And Brooklyn moved there permanently a few years ago."

Cole thought about it. The only reason he could see for moving somewhere so isolated was if someone was running from something. He certainly was, or at least using it to shape his life differently. But what could someone like Brooklyn be running from?

"I'd better go. Thanks for the coffee, bro. I'll be in touch soon."

"Good luck. And stop in any time."

"Let me know when Branson is back. I'm kinda worried about the guy."

"Me, too."

Cole stopped and gave Tori a kiss on the cheek, then made his way to the front door and put on his shoes.

Maybe he'd messed up the first two times he'd encountered Ms. Graves, but the third time could be the charm. And he knew just what he had to do to get past her thorny exterior.

CHAPTER THREE

THE DAY AWAY hadn't settled Brooklyn's thoughts, so she spent the next morning cooking. She did this every few weeks, making large quantities and then freezing in portion-size dishes. Cooking for one could be a lonely enterprise, but spending a day in the kitchen fed her soul as well as her body.

Today it was her grandmother's baked beans, done in her slow cooker, and fish cakes. She'd do them up and freeze them, and then fry a few off for tonight's dinner. Combined with the chow she'd just made this summer—a Maritime recipe of pickled green tomatoes—and she'd have the perfect dinner.

She was also making four small pans of lasagna, and a curried squash soup from the butternut squash in her garden.

As she put the squash in the pot, she figured she must be out of sorts indeed. This was enough food to feed her for weeks.

Her kitchen was a mess but the lasagnas were baking in the oven, the beans were bubbling, and it all smelled delicious. Two loaves of fresh bread were on the counter; mixing and kneading had helped her work out some of her frustration.

It was only eleven thirty when there was a knock and Marvin leaped up from his doggie bed, rushing to the door and barking the whole time.

It had to be Cole. There was literally no one else it could be.

She steeled herself, wiped her hands on her apron and went to the door. There was no sense pretending she wasn't home. Besides, she'd popped in to her lawyer's yesterday for a quick chat. She was going to look into the legalities and get back to Brooklyn in a few days. Even if Cole had the dock assessed, any work wouldn't start for a while.

She opened the door and tried to look polite.

"Hi," he said. "I come in peace."

She lifted an eyebrow. She couldn't escape the notion that there was always something behind his charm. "Oh?"

He held out his hands. One held a paper bag that she recognized from the baker in town. The other was from a pet store in Mahone Bay.

"Wine and cake for you, and something for Marvin, because he's a very good boy."

Okay, so charm aside, complimenting Marvin was the same as telling a mother her kid was great. It was the easiest way to get in her good graces. "I suppose you should come in, then." She stood aside.

Cole entered while Marvin danced in circles around him. She wished her dog didn't seem to like the guy so much. At first glance, Cole seemed to be dressed normally. Casually. Until she looked at the fine wool of his sweater and the rich leather of his shoes. There was no forgetting how stupid rich he had to be. After all, he'd bought most of the island and hadn't batted an eye at the idea of giving her a million dollars for her small corner of it.

"My God, it smells heavenly in here." He handed her the bag and then courteously removed his shoes and left them on the mat. "I heard you were a knitter. But apparently you're a cook, too."

She would not be charmed. She would not.

"It's messy at the moment. I tend to cook in batches and freeze it."

She put the bag on an empty space of counter and removed the wine and cake. A lovely crisp white, and a small but gorgeous lemon cream cake. She did love lemon.

"Thank you," she said, putting the wine in the fridge. "It wasn't necessary."

"But it was." He put his hands in his pockets. "Ms. Graves, we got off on the wrong foot, and that's my fault. What I should have said yesterday was that I would foot the bill for any changes to the dock. I'm the one who wants them, and it wouldn't be fair for me to ask you to pay half of that." He took a small step forward. "I know you aren't happy about me being here. But I promise, I'm not out to do you harm."

She wasn't sure what to say. He seemed very genuine and contrite.

"The previous owners and I got along very well," she admitted. "Before that, my grandparents owned the whole island. But then my grandfather got sick and needed a lot of care. Care he couldn't get here on the island, of course, and it put a financial strain on them. Ernest bought it, minus this parcel of land, and rented this house for two years before he built the grand house on the bluff. He set up the conditions for the shared dock and made sure we were taken care of. I understand why he sold. But it was a good relationship built on trust." She met his gaze evenly. "You haven't built up that trust."

"Yet," he said, and didn't smile. He seemed

to be taking everything she said very seriously. "Maybe if I tell you my plans for the property, it'll put your mind at ease."

The squash was nearly done, so she motioned toward the table and chairs. "I've got to finish this up, but please have a seat. Would you like a coffee?" There was still half a pot left.

"I'd like that a lot. Just black for me."

She poured him a cup and put it before him, and then went to test the squash and add the remainder of the ingredients. She tried to ignore how he was watching her as she poured the mixture over into her food processor and whizzed it until it was velvety smooth, and then poured it back over into the pot.

"What is that?" he asked. "It smells amazing."

"Curried squash soup. Do you cook, Mr. Abbott?"

He sighed. "Can we maybe forgo the formalities? Just call me Cole."

"All right." She didn't extend the offer to use her first name, though she suspected he would, eventually, anyway. She didn't want to be friends with him, but he had brought a peace offering and she appreciated his putting her mind at ease about the dock. Maybe, just maybe, she'd been a little hyper-defensive.

"Anyway," he continued, "I cook a little. But I'm better at buying stuff that's already prepped. I, uh, didn't really have to cook for myself growing up."

She snorted. "I kind of figured that about you. Let me guess. Private school? Trust fund baby?"

"Something like that." He shrugged. "But just to clarify, I've had to work my way to where I am. I absolutely had advantages because of family money. Hopefully I didn't waste any of them."

She turned around to look at him. There was something in the set of his jaw and behind his eyes that spoke of a deeper story. She wondered what it was. She should not dismiss him as an idle rich jerk. Everyone had their own story, didn't they?

"So buying this island...it isn't a whim or a toy for you?"

He shook his head. "No, it's not. I bought it for a few reasons. I'll tell you if you're interested in hearing about them."

He took a long drink of his coffee and Brooklyn looked at the clock. It was just shy of noon.

"I guess I'd better spoon up some of this soup then, shouldn't I?"

She reached into the cupboard for two bowls

and wondered if hearing him out was the right thing to do. Because right now it felt a bit dangerous.

Cole wasn't sure why he was ready to confide in Brooklyn or why he felt this pressing need to have her understand or think well of him. They'd got off to a rocky start and she certainly wasn't a friend or even someone he could really trust.

But he wanted to tell her, to disabuse the notion that he hadn't just bought the island as a toy or new thing on an acquisitions list. Besides, he was looking forward to hosting his first retreat in a few weeks, just a small gathering of executives from his own companies. Nothing formal, just four days of unplugging, sea air, good food. A time to slow down.

Brooklyn put a bowl of the delicious-smelling soup in front of him, and then went to the kitchen island and grabbed a loaf of fresh bread, a cutting board and a knife. She sliced it right there at the table, handed him a slice and put a crock of butter beside him.

The bread was still slightly warm and smelled like heaven.

"So. You have plans for the property. Do tell."

She got a second bowl and joined him at the table.

Cole went to work spreading butter on his bread. "A while ago I had a bit of a…well, I don't want to say a breakdown. It was more burnout, I guess. I'd been working sixty hour weeks for as long as I could remember, and then my social life… Well, I don't do anything half way. I'm not a partier or anything, but I'd do dinners and events and just… I never took any downtime." He broke off a piece of bread and popped it into his mouth. Amazing. A quick glance told him that Brooklyn was watching him intently, her eyes focused on his and her brow slightly furrowed as if she were trying to puzzle him out.

"Burning the candle at both ends," she said.

"Exactly. Until the flame got snuffed out. I was exhausted. Then one morning I woke up and I had chest pains. It scared the hell out of me."

She had picked up her spoon but now she put it down again. "Did you have a heart attack? But you're only what, thirty-five? Forty?"

He grinned. "Thirty-five, if you must know, and no, thankfully it wasn't a heart attack. It was a panic attack."

"Thank goodness," she said and picked up her spoon again.

He did the same and tasted the soup. It was velvety smooth and divine. He'd eaten in Michelin-starred restaurants and this simple soup could stand with the best of them. "This is amazing."

"It's the coconut milk. I stir a little in at the end, too, and it makes it pop." She looked at him over her spoon. "So, you had a panic attack."

"It wasn't an isolated thing. My friend Branson said that it was my body's way of telling me I needed to slow down and I needed to listen. I didn't have any choice. I could hardly get out of bed in the morning. I was tired all the time. I didn't believe him, you know? I thought I had some horrible disease. Turns out it was workaholism."

"So you bought the house."

"I'm getting there." He spooned up more of the soup like it was a tonic, which maybe it was. Simple, wholesome nourishment. Perfection. "It took me a long time to recover. Thankfully, I had strong executives in place, but the whole thing could have been avoided if I'd done a better job at balancing my workload. I didn't take time off until my own body forced me to. So I bought the house for a few reasons. One, it's a getaway for me, and one that is close to my two best friends, who bought places on the south shore. The other reason is that I don't want what happened to me to happen to other executives. I'm going to hold corporate retreats. First for my own people, and then for other companies."

He didn't mention how dark a place his burnout had been, though. How he'd felt so alone and questioned his existence. Wondering if anyone would miss him because other than Branson and Jeremy, he hadn't nurtured any relationships in his life. Especially romantic ones. His parents had put on a brilliant public face but in private they were strangers. If that was marriage, he didn't want any part of it.

Brooklyn frowned. "It's a neat idea, for sure. I'm going to be honest, though. It makes me uncomfortable thinking about strangers roaming about the island all the time." She stirred her soup as if deliberating something, then looked up again. "You're creating an oasis for people, which is admirable. But in doing so, you're threatening mine. It's a hard pill to swallow."

He hadn't thought of it that way. But of course. Every time he held a retreat, there would be strangers on the beaches, walking the island, on the boat launch. He could understand how that made her uneasy. Maybe it would convince her to sell to him after all?

And yet, the thought of her not being here, in this house, in this kitchen, suddenly seemed wrong.

"I'm sorry about that. It's definitely an unintended consequence. I guess it must seem as if I'm invading your home. That's not my intention at all. I hope you believe that."

She nodded but didn't meet his eyes. Instead she sliced him more bread. He got the feeling that it was more to keep her hands busy than anything.

He reached over and put his hand over hers. She stopped breathing.

Something changed in that moment, in that small but intimate physical touch. He felt it in his solar plexus, reaching in to grab him and hold him captive. It had been meant to reassure. But as her gaze darted to his, the energy between them became something bigger. Something unexpected.

She slipped her hand away from his. "Would you like more soup?"

It had rattled her, too. Cole cleared his throat and knew he'd better get out of there before he started sharing other things or, worse, inviting her to share. The idea was to convince her to sell. Not get himself tangled up in her.

"I should get back. I really just came with the peace offering."

Brooklyn gathered up their bowls and took them to the sink. "Thank you. And I appreciate the clarification on the dock maintenance."

Cole stood and brushed a few breadcrumbs off his pants. "I want us to deal fairly with each other. It's not my intention to cause you financial hardship."

She spun around and pinned him with a stare. "Don't worry about my financial situation. I'm doing just fine."

Dammit, he'd stepped in it again. Just when he'd let down his guard a little. "I'm sure you are. But no one wants an unexpected expenditure, do they?"

Marvin had reappeared and he leaned over to give the pup a pat and a bit of an ear rub. "You've got a great dog. I never had one growing up."

"But you like them." Her voice was softer. "That's pretty obvious."

"I do. Very much." Marvin leaned into a scratch, which delighted Cole immensely. "You're such a good boy, aren't you, Marvin? Mmm…that feels good."

When he looked up, Brooklyn was smiling. Damn, she was so beautiful when she smiled. He was going to have to step carefully there.

"He likes you, too. You can stop by for a game of fetch when you need to," she offered.

It was unexpected and he frowned. "Really? You're inviting me to play with your dog?"

She shrugged. "Dogs are great healers, Cole. From what you said, you probably need him as much as he needs a good game of throw-the-tennis-ball."

"Thanks," he said quietly, standing again. "Maybe I'll do that."

But as he said his goodbyes and made his way down the path from her house, he wondered what kind of recovery she'd needed, and if Marvin had been there for her. He hoped so. The thought of Brooklyn, such a strong, beautiful, independent woman needing some sort of healing made his stomach tie up in knots. If she'd had to recover from something, he hoped she hadn't had to do it alone.

CHAPTER FOUR

BROOKLYN KNEW THE day the executives arrived because the helicopter made an appearance, swinging low over the house before disappearing over the trees to the landing pad. She stepped away from the window and went back to printing shipping labels. She'd spent too much time thinking about Cole and that moment when he'd touched her hand. Something had happened between them, like a bolt of lightning. The startled look on his face had told her he had felt it, too. It made everything more complicated.

She should just brush it off and regain her common sense. But the past few nights, when she'd gone to bed, she'd lain awake thinking of how he'd brought Marvin a present and the way he patted the dog and rubbed his ears. Marvin was the most important thing in her life, really. As much as it would be more convenient for her to still hate Cole, his actions suggested an unexpected kindness and gentleness.

Kindness didn't translate into trust, though. He was a long way from accomplishing that.

Better to focus on the present. She needed to go over to the mainland again today. She'd finished dyeing another batch of yarn and had packed up new orders to be shipped away. Fall was a busy time for her. As the weather cooled, people picked up their knitting needles again and started on a number of projects. Even though it was only early October, Christmas orders were already flooding in.

She should forget about Cole and think more about the holiday season and building up her stock.

The seas were calm and the day clear, and the trip seemed to take no time at all. The first stop for her was the post office, which took a fairly long time as she had a number of shipments. Then she drove down to Liverpool to visit Delilah. Even though Brooklyn had her own yarn business, there were many specialty yarns that she sourced elsewhere. Right now she was hoping Delilah had a new shipment of alpaca yarn. She loved working with it, and her customers liked it, as well, since it was lighter than wool and wasn't scratchy.

Delilah was at the store but more than happy

to go to lunch. They headed to a local inn and dined on hearty chowder and fresh bread.

Delilah, who was in her midforties, took a look at Brooklyn and angled her head, as if assessing. "There's something different about you. A different kind of energy." She thought for a moment and shrugged. "You've perked up."

Heat slid up Brooklyn's neck. "I love the fall. It's my favorite time of year."

"I don't think so. What's going on in your life?" She leaned forward. "Have you put up that online dating profile like I suggested?"

Brooklyn laughed and spooned up more chowder. "No, I didn't. It's nothing, really. I mean, I met the new owner of the house. Otherwise I've just been busy." She raised an eyebrow. "After what I just spent at your store, you can tell I have orders piling up."

"What's he like? Is he old with a big paunch and stinking rich?"

She laughed, but the image of Cole standing at her door with cake and wine stuck in her head and her heart gave a little thump. "He's stinking rich, from what I gather. He's maybe thirty-five? And quite good-looking."

"Ooh. Some island romance in your future?" She waggled her eyebrows suggestively.

"Yeah, and wouldn't that be awkward. You

don't…you-know-what where you eat, Del. Besides, he'll be here a bit and then have to go back to New York. That's where his businesses are. He'll only be on the island now and again."

To her surprise, the thought made her a little lonely. She was used to having someone else for company. The summer hadn't been that bad, because the weather had been great and she'd had the gardens to keep and her own vegetable plot. In the wintertime, though, she often got storm-stayed. During those times, she'd often gone up to the big house with Ernest and Marietta and they'd played cards and eaten great food and it had been more than pleasant. Her house was cozy as anything, but the thought of facing the winter without any company at all… Maybe she should consider finding an apartment or something in town. But how could she afford two places? Right now she was mortgage-free and the business was more than enough to keep her comfortable. But if she had to add a thousand a month or so to her bills, it would make things tight.

She sniffed a little. A thousand a month was probably Cole Abbot's wine budget. Or whiskey, or scotch, or whatever pricey alcohol he drank. She'd looked up the wine he'd brought. She was used to the ten-to-twenty-dollar bottles. The one he'd brought had been sixty. She was saving it for a special occasion.

"So, young, rich, not a troll," Delilah said, ticking each attribute off on her fingers. "Remind me again why you're not making a move to tap that?"

Brooklyn snorted. "Thanks, Del, for getting right to the point."

"Any time." Her face softened, and she patted Brooklyn's hand. "Look, I just want you to be happy. And I know you don't need a man for that. I just worry that you… Well, you've closed yourself off to possibilities because of what happened."

Del was one of the few people who really knew about Brooklyn's trauma. Being a victim of a violent crime had changed Brooklyn, made her more wary and less trusting. Sure, she'd done all sorts of therapy and she was doing well. But she'd also built the life she wanted and didn't like the disruption.

She'd had enough counseling to understand that she liked guarantees. She wasn't a risk-taker, and in her mind, love was the biggest risk of all.

"It's not that, Del." She took a sip of her tea and sighed. "I mean, I'm not physically afraid of a relationship." The assault hadn't been sexual. It had been a straight up robbery, and looking back, it seemed like something from a movie. It certainly felt like it had happened to someone else. The fear had been cold and debilitating. The hard press of the gun dug into her ribs and she could still feel the painful grip of his big hand on her arm. For a few terrified moments, she'd been his hostage. But when he got into the car, she'd managed to scramble out the passenger side and he'd sped off. She'd been safe, yet forever altered.

"No, sweetie," Delilah said gently. "You're afraid of living. Everything happens in good time, but sometimes people come along that shake us up a bit." She smiled. "Maybe this guy is going to shake you up."

He already had. "He likes Marvin, and Marvin likes him back, the traitor," she confessed. "Then again, pats and treats go a long way with dogs."

Delilah grinned. "Not just with dogs. I'm partial to pats and treats myself."

"Delilah!" Brooklyn started to laugh and put down her teacup. Delilah had been married to the same guy for fifteen years and they were still adorable together. "This is why I love you."

"And here I thought it was because you get a bulk discount at the store."

"I'm nicer than that."

"I know that. I hope you do. Anyway, if this guy isn't going to be on the island that much, why not have a thing or see where it goes? God knows you deserve it."

Brooklyn had gone "home" to recover, really. The trauma from those five minutes in her life had resulted in crippling fear and panic. Life was much better now, but she didn't like change. Didn't want it.

Even one as sexy and intriguing as Cole Abbott.

When she returned home later that afternoon, she put her supplies in the house and took Marvin out for a walk on the beach so he could get a good romp in before the weather changed. The forecast called for rain later in the evening, and Brooklyn could feel the change in air pressure and humidity as she threw a stick of driftwood for Marvin. He was four now, and his energy level was still that of a puppy, though he definitely had more discipline. He came running back and dropped the stick at her feet, panting happily, eyes flashing as he waited for her to throw it again. She did, then walked on, the sharp wind buffeting her ponytail, pulling strands out to blow around her face, and puffing her jacket out behind her. The calm seas of earlier were now gray with little white caps. Tonight would be the perfect night to finish her shawl and then move on to holiday projects.

Delilah had given her food for thought. Not that she wanted to have a torrid affair or anything. It was more the reminder that she'd hidden herself away here.

She'd even withdrawn from her family. Her parents lived in Halifax, where her dad worked for a courier company and her mom was a nurse. Her brother and sister no longer lived in Nova Scotia; her sister was a geologist working in Alberta, and her brother an environmental engineer for a US company based out of Maryland. Brooklyn took the stick from Marvin and threw it again, watching him spin up sand as he chased after it. Brooklyn had been in her third year of her science degree when the assault happened. Then everything had changed.

She got to the end of the sandy stretch and climbed the path to the grassy expanse above. Darkening skies told her she should get home soon; she wasn't keen on getting caught in the rain, especially with Marvin and his wet dog smell. She called for him to come and was answered with a bark that sounded farther away than she anticipated. Frowning, she directed her gaze toward the sound of the bark and saw Marvin's golden coat running through the tall grass, headed toward Cole.

Not fair, considering Delilah's words still echoed in her head. Hopefully she could remain cool and detached and not blush.

Cole lifted a hand in greeting, and Marvin bounced and danced beside him.

"My dog is incredibly undisciplined," she said as he approached. "Sorry."

"Don't be. Marvin's great. I wish I'd had a dog as a kid. My folks said no because they are dirty and then pets aren't allowed in dormitories."

"Even for rich kids?"

He laughed. "Even for rich kids. Merrick was a great school. It's where I met Jeremy and Branson. But no dogs, sadly."

"Jeremy, as in your Realtor?"

He nodded. "Yes, that's right."

"And Branson is…"

"Branson Black."

She tried not to let her mouth drop open and failed. "The novelist."

"That's the one." Cole grinned. "We've been best friends since we were thirteen."

Brooklyn had been brought up in the city. All her classmates were God knows where. She'd made friends here, though. Good ones, like Delilah. Besides, in a small town, everyone pretty much knew everyone else.

Which meant most knew something about

why she'd moved home while in university and holed up on the island. It was a hard place to keep secrets.

"Aren't your guests on the island?" she asked, waving the stick for Marvin. She tossed it and he ran off, while Cole chuckled.

"They don't need babysitters. Right now they're settling in. Getting downtime." He grinned. "I confiscated their phones when they arrived. Cue looks of panic."

"That's torture." But she grinned in response.

"You would think so. I let each person send an 'I've arrived' message and then that's it for four days. Either people are napping, or working out, or trying to figure out a way to work without being connected. Switching out of that mindset is hard, and it takes time. We'll get together tonight at dinner."

"Cool." They walked on, down the path toward the lane that ran the length of the island from her house to his. Marvin trotted around with the stick of driftwood in his mouth, proud of his new possession. A gust of wind buffeted them and there was a bit of mist in it. The rain wouldn't be far off now.

"Looks like we're in for some nasty weather."

"Just some rain." She put her hands in her jacket pocket. "By tomorrow night it'll be clear again. But it was choppy on the water today. I hit some big waves on the way back."

"You're not scared doing that?"

She laughed. "I've been piloting around this island since I was old enough to see over the wheel. And when the weather is really bad, I stay home." She let out a sigh. "Honestly? Sitting by my window with a glass of wine, watching the rain? It's cozy and pretty relaxing."

"Hmm. I kind of wish I could do that tonight. Instead I'm going to try to deal with five VPs who are going through tech withdrawal."

She bit down on her lip. Had he just said he wanted to spend the evening with her, or had he been speaking theoretically? She tried to imagine Cole in her small living room and couldn't make it fit. Then she thought of the great room at the house, with the windows facing the water, and could totally picture him sitting there, swirling a brandy or something, watching the rain. A very different world from hers.

Their steps had slowed as they reached the lane. To the right was his house, gray and imposing, absolutely stunning. She'd been inside lots of times when Ernest had owned it, and wondered what sort of changes Cole had made to the decor. Maybe someday she'd get to see inside again. But not today. Today he was…well, if not working, he was busy with his guests.

"I meant to ask you. Do you know if Ernest had someone taking care of the grounds? I have my caretakers, but they had a few questions about what's in the shed and about a couple of the plants in the garden. If you knew who they could contact…"

She smiled. "Send them down to the house, or have them call me. I can give them the details."

"You don't have to do that."

"Cole, I looked after the grounds for Ernest. I love gardening. He paid me a monthly wage and I mowed the grass, tended his flower beds and did his snow removal."

Cole stopped and stared at her. "You did?"

She started laughing. "Did you think I had someone here to do it for me? Granted, my little flower beds and lawn are tiny in comparison, but if I want off the island in the winter I have to clear the lane so I can get to the dock. There's a nice little tractor up there with a blower attachment. Works great."

"Oh. Well." He stared a moment more, apparently still recovering from his surprise. "This monthly wage thing…" An awkward silence followed.

"I can live without it. I knew when Ernest sold the house that gig would come to an end. To be honest, Ernest was too old to do it all, and he wouldn't hear of me doing it without being paid. It worked for both of us."

"I see. I just don't want to deprive you of any income."

She lifted her chin. It was the second time he'd made that sort of comment to her, insinuating she was down on her luck. She was actually doing pretty well for herself. She had a new holiday pattern going up on a popular site this month, and because she'd built a solid reputation for accurate and clear pattern instructions, every time she sold a new pattern, she saw increased downloads.

One of the things she really wanted to do was put together her own book of patterns and find a publisher.

"I'm doing fine, thanks. Of course you should have your own employees take this over." And to be honest, it would feel strange, working for Cole.

"Raelynn would also like your recipe for that soup you made the other day. I raved about it."

"Oh, well, that's easy enough. As I said, send her down. I'm not headed anywhere for a few days."

"Thanks, Brooklyn. I appreciate it."

She looked over at him. "I suppose this means we're being friendly now." She deliberately used the verb instead of the friend noun. Acting friendly didn't necessarily constitute friendship.

"I suppose it does."

And he smiled.

He was pretty gorgeous at any time, but when he smiled it was something different altogether. His eyes got tiny crinkles in the corners and his whole body seemed to relax with it. Right now, in the gloominess of the coming rain, his eyes seemed grayish blue, but she'd noticed the other day in the sun that they were a clear, bright blue that seemed to look right inside her. Kind of like the ocean, changing color depending on the weather and the storms going on inside.

"You should get back to your guests. They're probably trying to figure out how to get internet on your TV."

He grinned again. "I turned off the Wi-Fi."

"Sneaky." She couldn't help but smile back.

"I know we'll be outside some, but I'll make sure we don't invade your privacy."

"Thank you. I appreciate it."

They said their goodbyes, but as Cole walked away, Brooklyn sighed. She almost wished he'd invade her privacy. She couldn't imagine making a move herself, and knew without a doubt he was not for her. And yet a part of her wished he might be, just a little. Even though he was exactly the wrong kind of man, and not at all what she needed.

CHAPTER FIVE

By the third day of their visit, Cole's VPs were bright and energetic and far more relaxed than he'd expected. Some of it he credited to the scenery, fresh air, the wonderful food that Raelynn provided to the group, and full nights of sleep. They'd taken the boat to the mainland today and had gone to the Sandpiper Resort for a delicious lunch. They'd stayed for two hours, talking about their respective divisions, brainstorming ideas in the casual setting. The downtime had refreshed them and Cole could feel the renewed excitement and energy around the table. It was exactly what he'd hoped to achieve.

Once they were back on the island, Cole turned on the Wi-Fi and they had an online session with an expert on balancing an executive workload with wellness to avoid burnout.

Cole looked at the group when the facilitator left the session. "So what did you think?

Tomorrow's our last day before you return to real life. What takeaways do you have?"

Duncan leaned forward and put his elbows on his knees. "I gotta tell you, Cole, when you took my phone I was pretty ticked off. But when I caught myself reaching for it over and over, I realized what an addiction it's become. I've become used to having it all the time, which means I'm always working. I think it's contributed a lot to my stress level. I still miss it." Everyone laughed a bit. "I'm trying not to go crazy wondering what's happened to the company in my absence. But I've slept better the last two nights than I have in months. Maybe years. I didn't realize how much I needed the break until I took it."

The other men nodded in agreement. "I found the first day and a half really hard," James added. "I don't know what it's like to have nothing to do...and then not have any tech to keep me from being bored. This was really like a work/tech detox for me, and one I can see I really needed."

Cole smiled, pleased at the feedback. "I know it's hard not to feel as if things are going to fall apart if you're unavailable, but they're not. If you have the right people in place, they all know their jobs. You can trust them. Nurture their talents. Have confidence in their abilities, which makes for better employees. And has the by-product of cutting you some slack. Look at me, for example." He looked at each man, right in the eye. "I'm the president and CEO. I took on responsibility for everything for a long time. But that's not sustainable and certainly not healthy. Instead I have great people in place who know their jobs.

"You guys, it starts with us. From the top down. I don't want to see any of you crash and burn out. It's not good for you, for your families, or for Abbott."

Everyone nodded thoughtfully.

"Tomorrow is our last day. I'd like for us to have a working breakfast midmorning where we can discuss your ideas for taking this back to not only your job but to your divisions. What changes you think would work with regards to your staff and their workload. Now that you've had a chance to unplug and get your creativity fired up again, let's see if we can leave with some action items. Sound good?"

They broke up and had a few hours until dinner, so two of the execs decided to take a walk on the beach, one was going to hit the gym, and the fourth had rediscovered a love of cooking and had agreed to help Raelynn with the dinner. Cole was left alone, pleased at how the day had gone, glad that he'd been able to give his own VPs a chance to decompress and recharge. If he'd done that now and again, he might have avoided the full-on breakdown.

It didn't really surprise him to find himself gravitating toward the rambling house in the trees. He hadn't spoken to Brooklyn since that day on the beach, though he'd seen her briefly this morning as they'd driven the golf cart from the house down to the dock. She'd been in her front yard raking leaves, her hair in a high ponytail and a pair of jeans hugging her backside.

Marvin was nowhere to be seen, but that was okay. He didn't need the dog to be chasing the cart or anything. Still, he'd wondered about her. What was she doing to fill her days?

He wandered toward her place, trying to think of an excuse for dropping in. He was nearly at her yard and still hadn't come up with anything plausible. Maybe he should turn around and go home again.

Instead he found himself on her front step.

He knocked. There was a flurry of barking, and then her footsteps as she came to the door and opened it.

Her hair was gathered up in a messy nest on the top of her head, and she wore a stained sweatshirt and sweatpants. "Oh. I'm sorry. I'm interrupting something, aren't I?" A strange, sharp odor permeated the air.

"I've been dyeing yarn the last few days," she answered. "That's the smell. Do you want to come in?"

He didn't want to intrude, but he was incredibly curious. How did someone hand-dye yarn? Marvin was standing just behind her, tail wagging, no longer barking in alarm but as if waiting to greet a friend. "Hey, Marv," he said, stepping inside. "I have to admit, I'm curious. I've never seen hand-dyed yarn before."

She led him through the house, to a back porch that had lots of natural light and counters. Several basins were lined up, and maybe four had dye inside and swirls of yarn soaking. On the other side of the room, drying racks were set up, with hanks of yarn lying across the wooden spindles. A small fan kept air circulating, and Cole spied one of the windows cracked open, even though the day was cool.

"This is it. My custom yarn business happens here," she said, tucking a stray piece of hair behind her ear. "I usually take three or four days and do a bunch at a time. Some are custom orders, and others are colors I've done before that are good sellers." She nodded at the drying racks. "Today I've done a lot of holiday ones."

Indeed. One looked like blocks of candy cane colors—red, white, green. "I didn't think of it being dyed in chunks of color," he said, wandering over toward the drying rack.

"When you ball it up, you'll see it's actually variegated. This one I call Peppermint Stick."

He grinned. "Cute."

"I do solid colors, too." She pointed at a deep, vibrant red. "That one is a big seller. This year I'm adding something new to my online shop, too. Kits. Comes with a pattern, the right amount of yarn, and any notions needed. I'm pretty excited about that."

"What sort of kit?" He was fascinated by the whole thing.

She picked up the red yarn. "A Christmas stocking, for example. This is a gorgeous color. I'll add some white with a pattern to knit a snowflake into the front and back. Then some white kind of trim for the top, and the pattern, and voilà. A home-crafted stocking for your mantel or as a keepsake for your kids or grandkids. I'll even include instructions for sewing in names with the white yarn."

"That's really, really neat." He was impressed. Even though her setup was low tech, clearly it worked fine. "Would it be easier if you had more space? You could do more at a time. How many can you dye in a day?"

"The rack holds five and I have two racks. Plus, the yarn has to sit in the dye for a good while, and then there's all the rinsing. I also only use eco-friendly dyes. It makes the cost go up a little, but my customers are willing to pay." She looked up at him, her eyes alight with enthusiasm. "Most people think of the fiber being sourced, but don't consider the dyes that are used in production."

She went over to the rack and picked up a circle of yarn. "When it's dry, like this is, I twist the hank into a skein." She deftly pulled the circle taut in her hands, started twisting it tightly and folded it in half so that it twisted around itself. Then she tucked one end inside the other and—poof!—it was done, just like that. "I put a tag on it and it's ready for shipping or knitting."

"You did that so quickly." He was still awed at the setup, and it wasn't just the fumes coming from the dye basins.

"I'll show you. Here."

She picked up another circle. "Okay, so put your hands inside the hank here."

"It's called a hank?"

"It is." She held his hands and spread them

until the yarn was tight. "Now, make an L with this hand, and use one finger on this hand."

She maneuvered his fingers and he tried not to think about how she was touching him. But she was in her comfort zone now, wasn't she?

"Okay. Now take this finger and make a twist."

He did. The motion and the thickness of the yarn made it awkward, but he twisted again, and again, each time a little more difficult as the twist tightened.

"Now bend your elbow and use it to halve the twist." She took his arm and helped him. The moment he bent the yarn, it wrapped around itself. He laughed. "Well."

"Seriously." She was smiling at him. "Now look. You tuck that end under so it stays together." She touched his hands again, helped him secure the skein. When it was done she smoothed it out. "Congratulations. You did it."

He grinned back at her. "It's really neat that you do this. That you make a living at it."

"It's an okay living. I'm a staff of one and my facilities are my great-grandma's summer kitchen, but it works." She met his gaze evenly. "I live a pretty simple life. I don't need much."

He respected that. Even admired it. It wasn't his life, and he wasn't sure he'd be good at that much simplicity. But how would he know? He'd never had the choice.

He held the yarn in his hands, the soft weight of it foreign and pleasant. "Well, I admire you. And I'm kind of jealous. I graduated and went right into business with my dad. A few years later he died, leaving me everything. I was kind of thrust into the role."

She took the yarn away from him and put it down on a table. "That sounds like a lot."

He nodded. "I was younger than you, and a sudden billionaire with a dozen companies to oversee. And I'd lost my father, so I didn't have him for advice or as a mentor."

He wasn't sure why he'd told her all that. It wasn't as if it was a secret; his dad's death had made the business pages and the news of his stepping into the CEO position had followed. But that last part…it made him feel a little bit vulnerable. He wasn't sure anyone understood what an adjustment it had been. How scared he still was of failing.

And how his dad had shared his business acumen but hadn't really taught Cole what it was like to be a man. Numbers and figures had been his way of communicating, but never anything personally meaningful. Anything he'd learned in that regard, he'd learned from his best friends.

"But you did it. And are a tremendous success," she reminded him quietly.

"I had the support of the directors, which helped." At least with the numbers and figures. Not so much with the loneliness.

"Until you crashed."

"Until I crashed."

She was very close to him now, close enough he could touch her if he wanted. And he wanted. It wasn't the smart thing but he was kind of tired of always feeling pressure to do the smart thing. Or the most fiscally responsible thing. He wanted a chance to be human. Mess up. Get his hands dirty.

"Cole," she said softly, and he realized he'd been staring at her lips like a fool.

"You are definitely not what I expected," he murmured, shifting his gaze from her mouth to her eyes. "Not at all."

"Nor are you," she replied, and her words were a little breathless. "But this isn't a good idea."

"I know. I'm not sure how much I care, though."

They'd drifted closer together until they were nearly touching. Cole held his breath as his heart pounded. And then he decided to abandon all caution and just do what he wanted to do—kiss her.

He curled a hand around the nape of her neck and leaned in, touching his lips to hers. They were soft and warm and opened a little in surprise, and she let out a small breath as he fit his mouth over hers more securely. She lifted her hand and let it rest on his arm, holding on and yet still holding back, just a little. She tasted like tea and cinnamon and vanilla, an intoxicating blend that made him think of home—or at least the home he hadn't had but always imagined.

All too soon he shifted back, not wanting to press his case, or go too fast. There was something fragile about her he couldn't put his finger on. Oh, she wouldn't break. She was a strong, stubborn woman. But there was something else, a vulnerability, that he sensed in her sweetness and hesitation.

"Oh, my," she said softly and bit down on her lower lip. It was so sexy he nearly groaned.

"I should probably get back. Everyone is leaving tomorrow, and Raelynn is cooking a farewell dinner tonight. Lobster's on the menu."

"Sounds lovely." She took a step back, then frowned a bit. "Listen, Cole…this probably isn't a good idea. I mean, you want to buy my house. Something between us muddies those waters. And I don't plan to sell, which means we'll be neighbors. Also awkward. So as much as I'm flattered…"

"No more kissing?" He was profoundly disappointed. He'd enjoyed kissing her very much. She was a thorn in his side, but he was starting to like her a lot. She was, as Tori liked to say, "good people."

"No more kissing," she confirmed. She shoved her hands into her sweatshirt pockets, a telling bit of body language he was curious about. Withdrawing and also protective…she didn't have to be afraid of him, though. He would never hurt her.

"I won't lie. I'm disappointed. But if that's what you want…"

"It is, yes. But it might be nice if we stayed on friendly terms. It does make living on the island together easier."

"Because you're not going to sell." He nearly smiled, but tried not to.

But she did, a sweet little uptick of the corners of her mouth as her eyes sparkled at him. "Because I'm not going to sell."

He nodded, then felt compelled to add, "You know that what I am willing to pay would set you up in a house and leave capital left over to run your business properly."

"But it isn't home. And right now…this is home."

She was definitely attached, and he couldn't honestly say he blamed her. There was something warm and inviting about the old house, and he'd already found himself captivated by the island.

"So I don't get the real estate deal and I don't get kisses. It seems I'm getting the rotten end of this deal."

She nodded, a sober expression on her face. "It appears you are," she replied, and damned if they weren't flirting after all.

"I'll just have to come up with a better offer." He held out a hand and gestured toward the door. "Shall we? I really do need to get back."

She led him to the front door. Marvin looked up from his doggy bed and his tail gave a thump, but he didn't get up and rush over. It was almost as if he was used to seeing Cole there. Like Cole somehow…belonged.

That was ridiculous, wasn't it? This was just a dog, and a slightly tired old house, and not his life at all.

"Helicopter tomorrow," he warned Brooklyn. "Fastest way to get my people from here to the airport."

"Thanks for the warning," she said, smiling a little. "Have a good dinner with your guests."

He almost wanted to invite her to join them.

Also ridiculous, but he was prolonging their goodbye and didn't know why.

So he said goodbye and went back to the graveled lane, toward the big house on the bluff.

Brooklyn kept her eye on the forecast as the week progressed. A midseason hurricane had formed to the southeast and was spinning its way north. The US eastern seaboard looked to be getting a miss, but Nova Scotia was another story, if the models were accurate. Right now it could go a little either way. A direct hit would be nasty. A bit to the right would bring lots of rain. To the left, crazy winds. Either way, it was a category three now, and they'd had a very warm autumn. Maybe it would only be a tropical storm when it hit, but right now forecasters were predicting a category one.

Which didn't sound that bad. Except she'd seen what even a category one could do. Widespread power outages. With her generator, that wasn't a huge deal. But the seas would be whipped up and rolling, which meant getting to the mainland would be out of the question. Her little boat wasn't up to it. She'd have to make a trip over and stock up on anything she might need.

Her needles clacked and she grinned. Wine, chocolate, dog food...all the necessities for being storm-stayed.

She spread the shawl out over her lap and admired the fine, even stitches and the soft yarn. This might be her favorite piece ever, and that was saying something. She imagined wrapping herself up in it this winter, with a cup of hot cocoa and a good book or DVD. She'd have Marvin for company, as always. And yet as she picked up the knitting again, a sense of unease slid through her. Cole would be gone, wouldn't he? And she'd be alone on the island. Not that she minded; she was used to it. But he wouldn't be here. With his smiley face and teasing voice and...well, just everything.

She'd gotten kind of used to him, after all. He made things interesting.

Her cell rang and she reached over to grab it, looked at the number, and frowned. It was a number that she didn't recognize at all. "Hello?"

"Hey, Brooklyn, it's Cole."

"You got my phone number." She wasn't sure if she was pleased or not.

"I got it from Jeremy, my Realtor, who had it because of...well. When I was trying to buy your house from under you."

She laughed out loud at his bluntness. "Fair enough. What's up?"

He was calling her. *Calling her.* It shouldn't make her giddy, but there were a whole list of *shouldn'ts* where Cole was concerned and she had so far ignored every single one.

"I'm having a dinner at my house tonight with my friends. Jeremy and Tori are coming over, and Branson is back in town with Jessica. I hate being a fifth wheel, so I wondered if you'd like to join us."

Oh, my. She wasn't sure if he meant for this to be as his date or if she was a chair filler. And she had no idea how to ask, either. "Dinner? With your friends? But I don't know them. Won't it be awkward?"

"Naw. It's just casual. They haven't been over to the island since I moved in, and I thought it would be nice to do it now since it looks like we're in for some weather later in the week."

She hesitated.

"Of course, if you don't want to, that's fine. I know it's last-minute."

Which was a paltry excuse because living somewhere with a population of two pretty much guaranteed an open social calendar.

"I could probably come. I guess."

"Great! Come any time after six. We'll have

pre-dinner drinks. Everyone's spending the night, so we can all indulge a little."

Oh, my. What had she agreed to? A cozy little dinner party with a bunch of billionaires, and her with a solid low five-figure income, no degree, no prestige…what would they have to talk about? When it was just her and Cole, she tended to forget he was so rich and accomplished. She was suddenly having second thoughts.

"Don't even think about backing out. I can hear your brain turning."

"Who said I was having second thoughts?" If she was good at anything, it was bluffing. Bluffing being strong, bluffing being independent, bluffing being…whole. But that was another story and one she was not planning to share with Cole.

He just laughed lightly. "Raelynn is cooking up a feast. Come hungry."

"Should I bring anything?"

"Just yourself. See you at six."

He was gone before she could say another word. It was fine. She'd met Tori before, and she was lovely. And it was just dinner. She could excuse herself if it was too much and walk home. Besides, she was curious to see what changes Cole had made. Ernest had had a decorator do the house, and she'd always thought the furniture a little heavy and dark. Had Cole kept the same vibe or done something very different? She knew he'd done some renos, but the work crews hadn't been there a very long time.

She put the knitting away and decided to take a bath and think about what to wear. She was having dinner with not one but three billionaires, wasn't she? And Jeremy's wife and Branson's girlfriend. There was no question that she was Cole's date. Even though it was a casual "round out the table" date, they were still paired up.

Second thoughts bubbled up again.

The bath and lavender salts helped to relax her, and she dressed in black leggings and her favorite long sweater that she'd knit herself, with drop sleeves and a V-neck. It was knit out of cashmere in a pinky-red rhubarb shade, and she slid on her favorite boots, brown leather ones that were well loved and classic, stopping at just below her knee. There was a bit of a debate in her head about wearing her hair up or down, but she decided to put it up in a top knot because she liked how it emphasized the V-neckline.

And because her clothing choices were still somewhat casual, she took extra time with makeup, going a little heavier than usual with her eyes and then a neutral lip. When she was done she pressed a hand to her stomach to calm her nerves. Dinner. It was dinner, for Pete's sake. Not an actual date. Not really. They weren't going to be alone or anything.

There was an odd little beep outside her house and she peered out the window. One of the golf carts was parked out front, and the man behind the wheel had to be Raelynn's husband, who worked as the caretaker. She laughed out loud. Even on this tiny island, Cole had somehow managed to send a driver to get her.

She went outside and approached, smiling at the man sitting patiently. "Hi, I'm Brooklyn."

"Dan," he replied, grinning back.

"Dan, I just need to let my dog out before I go. Do you mind waiting?"

"Of course not. I've heard about your dog. Cole talks about him."

"He does?"

He nodded. "My dad says that Cole was never allowed to have a dog at the house, but he always liked them. The Abbott house wasn't one for…well, I don't know. It was a bit sterile."

She filed that tidbit away, but what he'd said prompted another question. "Your father knows Cole?"

"He was Cole's father's chauffeur for years. I spent most of my childhood near the Abbotts."

Interesting. Brooklyn wondered why Cole had then hired Dan. Keeping it all in the family?

There was no time to ask, nor did she want to pry. Instead she went to let Marvin out, and once he'd had a pee and said hello to Dan, she put him back inside and slid into the cart. "Shall we?" she asked.

The sun was fading and there was a distinct chill in the air, though it wasn't what Brooklyn would call cold. It took no time at all and they were at the house. Lights glowed from the windows, and Dan dropped her by the front door. "Let me know when you want to go home, Ms. Graves."

"Please, call me Brooklyn. It's a small island and we should all be friends."

He smiled at that, a big genuine smile. "All right. Anyway, just let me know. There's no need for you to walk home in the dark."

She appreciated it, though she fully planned to walk. She knew this island like the back of her hand, dark or light. And there was something magical about being on an island, surrounded by the Atlantic, and looking up at the stars. It was awesome and humbling.

He drove away and Brooklyn was left with her next dilemma. Knock? Or let herself in? With Ernest, she'd always just knocked and stuck her head in the door, calling out. They'd had that sort of relationship. It was different with Cole, so she lifted the door knocker and rapped it smartly against the huge solid wood door.

CHAPTER SIX

THE DOOR OPENED and Raelynn smiled out at her. "Brooklyn! I'm so glad you came."

An ally. Brooklyn smiled back. She'd met Raelynn days earlier, when she'd come up to the house to chat about the gardens and Raelynn's plans for winter upkeep. The New Yorker was quick to learn and really entertaining. Brooklyn had laughed more in her company than she had for ages.

"Me, too. Dan picked me up. He's a nice guy, your husband."

Raelynn blushed. "We've been together for about six years. When Cole hired us to work as a team, well, it was a dream come true."

The couple wouldn't stay on the island in Cole's absence but would travel back ahead of him when the house was open. Apparently they'd be the ones maintaining everything during the retreats when Cole wasn't present, too. When Raelynn had told her that, Brooklyn had realized how much Cole must like and trust them.

Raelynn stepped aside. "Come on in, and I'll get you a glass of wine."

"That sounds lovely."

Together they walked through the foyer. Brooklyn expected to see Cole and his company seated in the vast living room, but instead laughter came from the kitchen. She entered and Cole's gaze found hers, his eyes lighting up with pleasure.

"You're here! Everyone, this is Brooklyn, my favorite neighbor. Brooklyn, this is Jeremy and Tori, their baby, Rose, and Branson and Jessica."

Jeremy reminded her a little of JFK Jr., only with shorter hair, and Branson...well. His nearly black hair tumbled over his collar and he looked a bit like a sexy pirate. She could see why Jessica stared at him with stars in her eyes. Tori and Jessica were both lovely in a way that made Brooklyn comfortable and not awkward. Maybe she'd expected them to be different—more coiffed and manicured, perhaps. Instead Tori snuggled Rose on her arm and smiled widely, her hair in slight disarray, and Jessica had the most adorable smile and freckles on her nose.

"I'm your only neighbor, so thanks for that dubious distinction. I'm very pleased to meet you all. Well, Tori and I have met before, briefly. It's good to see you again." She thanked Raelynn when she was handed a glass of wine. "Welcome to Bellwether Island."

"I hope Cole hasn't been a jerk," Jeremy offered. "When he sets his mind to something, he goes after it."

Her face heated but she hid behind taking a sip of wine before she answered. "Not at all. He knows my position on selling and so the subject is dropped. We've become friends." She smiled sweetly. Very sweetly.

Branson burst out laughing. "You were right, Cole. She's a firecracker."

Tori came over and touched her arm. "Good for you. Cole needs someone to put him in his place from time to time."

Jessica was grinning, leaning against Branson's arm. "I think you're pretty great," she said. "It takes a tough cookie to live out here full time."

The warm welcome was a pleasant surprise, so Brooklyn smiled and relaxed a little more. "You're a painter. I don't know if anything on the island inspires you, but you're welcome anytime."

Jessica nudged Branson. "See? That's what

you should have said when I showed up at your lighthouse."

Branson rolled his eyes and everyone laughed.

Raelynn was working behind them and finally shooed them out. "Okay, you bunch. I have work to do in here and you're in the way. Starter course in ten minutes."

Starter courses. It reminded Brooklyn of the fact that in her life, a starter course meant maybe a platter of vegetables and dip before a meal. How many courses would there be?

They moved into the living room and Brooklyn paused at the threshold. Cole had definitely decorated differently than his predecessor. While the glow of the lamps threw a warm and welcoming light, the color scheme was vastly different from Ernest's. Instead of cream and gold and brown, the room was painted a light gray, with a darker gray sofa and chairs, a glass-topped coffee table and a massive rug that covered the floor in shades of gray, blue and white.

It reminded Brooklyn of the gray waves and white caps of the ocean on a blustery day, brought inside, and she loved it. It was an extension of the landscape, blending in rather than keeping it out.

"Do you like it?" Cole asked, once he saw her face.

"I do. It's very different from what was here before. But it suits the house and...you."

"Thank you." He smiled at her. "Did you want another quick tour? I've made some other changes. I nearly forgot that of course you would know what it was like before."

She was curious. "I'd like that. But we can do it another time. You have guests."

He waved a hand. "They'll be fine for five minutes. Come on."

He'd taken a den and made it into a boardroom, complete with a huge table and executive chairs, and some sort of smart board. "Some of our retreats will be team building or brainstorming getaways."

The common areas had all been repainted into that same restful gray, cool and relaxing. Artwork decorated the walls, though Brooklyn didn't recognize any particular artist. In the main areas, the artwork was black-and-white: driftwood and dunes and cliffs. Cole had moved in and brought the ocean with him, and she had to say she loved it a lot. It felt fresh and modern and yet peaceful, with an underlying energy she couldn't quite pinpoint but made her feel grounded and strong.

"Did you have a decorator?"

"Yes." He led her up the stairs. "I brought in someone from New York. I think he did a good job, don't you?"

"It fits. It fits this island, and you, too. I loved it when Ernest lived here, but this is even better, I think."

"I'm glad you approve."

She looked up at him. "Oh, get real. You don't really care if you have my approval or not."

He tilted his head and met her gaze. "You know, that should be true. But lately I find myself caring about what you think very much."

"Cole..."

"I know. I'm just saying. Somehow I don't want to disappoint you."

After a tour of the guest rooms, he took her down and showed her the gym. By that time, Raelynn was calling them to the dining room, and she let out a sigh at the beautiful table setting.

There were three bowls with fresh flowers on the table, lending their sweet scent but low enough that the blooms didn't impede anyone's view of each other. Rose had started to fall asleep and was now sitting in a carrier nearby, covered with a blanket and staring dazedly at a bar holding very colorful and interesting shapes.

The table had had the extension leaves taken out of it so that it sat six. Cole was at the head and Jeremy at the foot, with Jessica and Branson on one side, and then Tori on an angle to Jeremy and Brooklyn on an angle to Cole. They were definitely paired up, but Brooklyn couldn't bring herself to mind. They all seemed to get along so well that it didn't matter anyway.

The first course was a ginger-carrot soup, perfectly seasoned with ginger and a hint of cumin and cayenne. Brooklyn decided to ask Raelynn for the recipe, and then the cook returned with asparagus wrapped in Parma ham. It nearly looked too pretty to eat with the vibrant green and crisp pink of the ham, and went perfectly with the dry Riesling Raelynn had poured during the soup course. The starters had been simple but delicious, and Brooklyn savored each bite as conversation flowed easily around the table.

Brooklyn was already wondering how she was going to make it to the main course when a small plate was placed before her, containing a kale and apple salad with pumpkin seeds and pomegranate arils. She looked up at Cole and said, "Where did you ever find Raelynn? She's a fantastic chef."

He grinned. "I'll tell her you said so. She

was working for a caterer and ran a party for my mother maybe six years ago. Incidentally, she also met Dan that night. She stayed with the caterer even after she and Dan married, and when I bought this place, I offered them the caretaker jobs."

Jessica put down her fork. "They don't mind being so isolated?" She looked at Brooklyn and smiled. "Not that it isn't lovely, but when someone is so used to the city, this can be a bit of a shock."

"None taken," Brooklyn replied. "It is isolated. Even for me, and I've pretty much been here my whole life." She thought about Raelynn and Dan living above the garage. She was sure Cole had it decorated nicely for them, but she understood now why he'd thought buying her out would provide them with a home of their own.

"They won't stay all year round," Cole said. "Only when it's required. And maybe through the summer." He leaned back in his chair, toying with his wineglass. "I'd like to be here in the summer months more. Enjoy the beach, maybe do some deep-sea fishing."

Jeremy laughed. "Look at you, slowing down."

Cole lifted an eyebrow. "And you, settling down. Whatever, bro."

Everyone laughed a little, and then Branson said, "That's not in the cards for you, Cole?"

Unease settled in Brooklyn's stomach. She was here as Cole's date, after all. She tried to keep a relaxed posture, even though the question seemed rather pointed, and did and didn't involve her at the same time. But Cole just shrugged easily. "Dude, you know me. I have too much going on, even if I have slowed down a bit. You and Jeremy can carry that flag. The single life works for me."

Jeremy gazed into Tori's eyes. "I'm definitely okay with that."

"Me, too," Bran said, leaning over and kissing Jessica's temple.

It was so obvious to Brooklyn that the other two couples were deeply in love. What in the world was she doing here? It had become horribly awkward. She suddenly felt like nothing more than a seat filler.

Thankfully, Raelynn returned with their main course, a maple-glazed salmon with tiny smashed potatoes and steamed vegetables. Brooklyn couldn't remember ever sitting down to such a feast. It was so different from her actual life, but everyone else was acting as if this happened every day. Did they always live like this?

There was a new wine for the salmon dish,

a pinot noir that was delicate and lighter than she normally liked her reds, but matched the salmon beautifully. Dear heaven, actual wine pairings in addition to all this food. And this was a "casual" dinner! She couldn't imagine what fancy would entail.

It was Jessica who totally switched gears and eased the knot in Brooklyn's stomach. "Brooklyn, I love your sweater. Is that cashmere?"

She nodded and smiled. "Thank you, and yes, it is."

"Did you make it yourself? Tori tells us you run your own knitting business."

Brooklyn glanced at Tori, who was smiling at her. Sure they'd met, but she was surprised that she'd been a topic of conversation. "What?" Tori asked. "People in town know who you are. Anytime you put something in the store in Liverpool, it goes like hotcakes. My mom actually downloaded one of your patterns for a baby blanket last winter."

"Oh, I hope it turned out! Which one?"

"The lacy carriage blanket. She said it knit up like a dream."

Jessica jumped in again. "I think it's beautiful. You'd pay through the nose for something like that in Manhattan."

Brooklyn chuckled. "I can't imagine there being a market for hand knits in Manhattan."

Cole stepped in. "Actually, you might be surprised. A little market research would tell you for sure."

"Which sounds a lot like big business. I'm pretty happy running my little one as it is, and on my own time."

She took a bite of the salmon and wondered why her heart was beating so fast. Everyone was so friendly and lovely, so why was she feeling like a complete fish out of water?

Branson was the one who stepped in. "Actually, I think Jess and I get that. What you do is very creative. It's not always a great idea to commoditize our creativity."

"Exactly." Brooklyn smiled at him and let out a slow breath. "I don't mind living simply if it means keeping my joy."

"Amen," Jessica said.

The subject changed again and Brooklyn focused on enjoying the flavorful main course. By the time dessert arrived, she wasn't sure she could eat another bite, until her serving of crème brûlée was placed in front of her.

She looked up at Raelynn. "You are evil, Raelynn."

Raelynn laughed. "Thank you. I'll take that as a compliment."

"You should. This is my favorite dessert."

She knew she shouldn't indulge anymore.

But she couldn't resist as she took her spoon and broke through the crust to the custard below.

It was nothing short of heaven.

After dinner, they all retired to the living room again. A fire had been laid in the fireplace and it crackled merrily. Tori went to their guest room and put a now sleeping Rose to bed. Brooklyn wasn't sure she should stay much longer. She was not a part of this group. It was clear that Cole would have been fine without a dinner partner, so why had he invited her? Why had he kissed her in her grandmother's porch? What did he even want? She knew what his purpose for the island was, but that was all. That was professional. And perhaps a little personal, but she had no idea what his motives were.

And yet she didn't believe he was playing games, either. He didn't seem the cavalier type.

Maybe she should just ask him. But not now. Not when his guests were curled up on his expensive furniture.

"I really should be going," she said with a smile. "But thank you for inviting me and for such a lovely dinner. I don't need to eat now for a week!"

Cole looked up, a frown appearing between his eyebrows. "So soon? It's only nine."

"I've got to be up early in the morning. This time of year I start getting a lot of orders. I don't want to fall behind."

"You must be getting a lot of holiday business starting," Tori said. "How do you keep up? Don't you worry about having carpal tunnel after knitting so much?"

"So far so good," Brooklyn replied. "But yes, this is a really busy time of year. It was so nice meeting you all and joining you for dinner, though." And she meant it. She'd felt awkward, but it wasn't because of anything anyone had said or done, not really. It was just an awareness that they lived in a world that was foreign to her.

"I'll call Dan to run you down," Cole said.

"No, please don't. It's a beautiful night and I'll walk."

"I'll walk you, then."

She was aware that the other two couples were hanging on their every word. "It's okay, Cole. You stay with your guests."

"Oh, we're fine," said Tori lightly. "We can spare him for half an hour."

"See?"

She wasn't going to win, and to protest further would only make it more awkward. "All right, then."

They headed out into the evening. With the

sun now down and the moon rising, the air had taken on a distinct chill. She hadn't thought she'd need a jacket over her sweater, but it was colder than she'd expected. Probably because the sky was perfectly clear, with a blanket of brilliant stars above them.

"Wow," Cole said, pausing on the gravel in front of the house. "You can see forever when there's no light pollution."

"Right?" She hugged her arms around herself and tilted her head to stare into the darkness. "There are a million stars tonight."

He was closer to her than she realized, because when he spoke again she jumped, startled by his nearness and how his soft voice was so close to her ear. "Stars make me feel both incredibly small and also like I belong to something vast. That probably doesn't make sense."

But it did make sense to her. She'd often felt the same. "When my brother and sister and I were kids, we used to lie on the sand and stare up at the stars." She laughed as the memory came rushing back. "My mom hated it because we always ended up with sand in our hair and bites from sand fleas on our legs and arms. It was my grandma who washed out all the little grains of sand and put calamine lotion on so we wouldn't scratch."

She turned her head and looked up at him.

There was a small smile on his face but his eyes seemed sad. "What?" she asked.

"Nothing. I just never did anything like that as a kid. Of course, I didn't have brothers or sisters, either."

Brooklyn thought it sounded unbearably lonely, and that those kinds of memories were something not even privilege could buy. "Then come on," she said impulsively, taking his hand and pulling him off the graveled path.

Cole let Brooklyn drag him along because he was simply enchanted by her. He had been, all through dinner. She'd shown up looking so incredibly beautiful, with her hair gathered up and the graceful curve of her neck exposed. He'd thought about what she might do if he kissed her right where her neck met her shoulder, if she'd sigh a little or break out in goose bumps. She'd enjoyed dinner, too. He'd stolen looks at her as she'd tasted each dish, sipped the wine that Raelynn had chosen for each course. It was a casual dinner with friends but to her it had been special, hadn't it?

Even the question about his single status hadn't fazed him...much. And that was surprising.

Now she was pulling him through tall, crackly grass as they made their way to the beach, ignoring any path. No matter where he was on the island, he could hear the ocean, but the shush of the breakers now reached his ears, and something built in his chest, something unexpected that he wasn't sure what to do with.

In this moment, he didn't want to be anywhere else but here, with her. Especially with her. And that complicated things so much. He did dates. He didn't do…more.

"Come on," she said, jumping down over a small dune and into the sand. She took off her footwear and left it at the edge, and let go of his hand as she danced toward the water. She was maybe ten feet away from the waves when she stopped, opened her arms wide and lifted her face to the sky.

Oh, damn. This wasn't a little complication; it was a huge one that he wasn't sure what to do with.

She spun around and called to him. "Come on!"

He took off his shoes and socks, and the cool sand squidged between his toes. He'd gone business casual tonight, so he was wearing nice trousers and a tailored button-down. Not exactly beach attire. She trotted back and grabbed his hand. "Come on, slowpoke. We're going to look at the stars."

He laughed and followed her, and then to his surprise, she dropped down onto the sand and made to lie down.

"Wait!" He stopped her as he shrugged out of his jacket. "We can put this under our heads. So we don't get sand."

Her smile was wide as she took his jacket, then spread it on the sand. "Okay, come on down."

He wasn't sure if he'd get any fleabites... after all, this was Nova Scotia in early October. Wouldn't it be too cold or something? And right now he didn't actually care. He lay down on the sand beside her and put his head on his jacket. They had to lie close together to share the "pillow," and he liked the feeling of her body next to his.

"Look up," she said, her voice barely more than a breath, and he opened his eyes to the sky above.

It was so big. Inky blackness stretched endlessly, with thousands of stars blinking at them. The ocean swept in and out, lulling him into relaxing. And yet he was so very aware of the woman beside him that it was impossible to relax completely. He sensed her every breath and could smell her floral shampoo. And when she reached out and hooked a few of her fingers in his, his chest tightened.

Brooklyn Graves was a beautiful woman. Not just outside, but inside, too.

"Look," she whispered, pointing up with her free hand. "There's a satellite moving across the sky."

The silver light moved in a precise arc and he watched it for several seconds. "Do you know the constellations?"

"Not really," she replied. She slid her fingers away and he missed the contact. "I mean, I know the Big and Little Dippers. But the rest... I like making things up instead. Kind of like when you see shapes in the clouds? I like to find them in the stars."

God, she was so pure, wasn't she? How many women had he met in his lifetime who would indulge in a bit of whimsy to make up their own constellations? It struck him that maybe he'd spent a lot of his time with the wrong sort of woman.

And wondered if that was because of the example set at home. His mother had not been a nurturer. It was something that he and Jeremy had in common. Jeremy had had a stepdad. Cole had still had his father, but his father had barely been around. His first love was always Abbott Industries. And when his will had been read, his instruction to his son was "Please don't ruin my company." Nothing about being happy or finding love...and when Cole had looked at his mother's impassive face at the cemetery, he'd wondered if they'd ever loved each other at all.

He let out a long breath, wishing he knew how to let go of the past. But it popped up now and again, and more often lately. He couldn't imagine living in a loveless marriage—or worse, loving someone only to have them stop loving you.

Especially when you weren't really that lovable to begin with.

"That was a 'deep thought' kind of sigh. You okay?"

He felt her gaze on his profile and stared at the stars. "Yeah, I'm fine. Just thinking."

"What about?"

"My family." He debated whether or not he should say more. He didn't talk about his personal life. But there was something about Brooklyn that invited him to be open. "My mother would never have done this. Neither would my dad. To be honest, I'm not even sure why they had me. I spent my whole life trying to gain their approval, or rebelling at never getting it. Now it's too late anyway."

"Even for your mother? I know your dad is gone, but she's still living, right?"

"Yeah. We don't have much of a relationship. She wasn't very maternal."

"I see."

"I spent a lot of time looking for validation, and not enough time actually living. Being here on the island has hammered that home, and sometimes I'm not sure what to do with it."

"It sounds like you made a lot of life changes after your health scare."

"Let's call it what it is. I had a breakdown. Of course it was all kept super quiet, because if it had gotten out, Abbott stock would have plummeted."

"That's a lot of pressure to put on a single person, Cole."

He didn't answer, because she was right.

"So what are you going to do? Walk away?"

"No." That he was able to answer definitively. "I do know I have to stop being self-destructive. Being a workaholic is not the answer. But I still need to have a purpose and a reason to be busy. I can't just hide away here. It's nice for a little while, but not forever."

"Balance."

"Yeah. It's one of those words that get thrown around a lot, but for me it means making sure I take time out, that I don't burn out, that I don't have to do everything myself. It sounds like it should be easy, but when you've lived that way your whole life, the habits are hard to break."

He'd been on the island a few weeks, and he was already getting antsy to get back. He did actually like his job. He liked building things and helping people and solving problems. And so far he had not ruined the company. On the contrary.

"You have wonderful friends who support you." She nudged a little closer and he wondered if she was cold.

"Here," he said, sitting up a bit and holding his arm out. "You're cold. Snuggle in."

She hesitated for a moment, then just when he thought she was going to say no, she slid closer and let him pull her next to his body. She fit there so well. Made him want things he'd never wanted in his life.

They stargazed a few minutes more, silent but for the waves slipping over the sand. He wondered what he should do. He could send her home and say he needed to get back to his friends. He could walk her home and say good-night, and be a gentleman. He could turn toward her and kiss her soft, full lips, even though they'd agreed they would not be sharing kisses again.

He should send her home. Get back. Forget about this impulsive beach trip and make plans to head back to New York soon. She wasn't the kind of woman he could or should play games with.

He rolled to his side so he was facing her and rested his head on his hand, braced by his elbow.

Her lips twitched. "You're supposed to be looking at the stars."

"I'm looking at something more beautiful than stars."

"There's a line."

"It's not a line if it's true."

She turned her face toward him. "What do you want, Cole?"

He struggled with how to answer. He couldn't lie. He couldn't say nothing, and he couldn't say more than he felt. So he let his gaze lock with hers as he admitted, simply, "You."

Her chest rose and fell with a big breath, and her eyes widened. "But that's all, right? You're not looking for a relationship or a girl-friend or whatever."

"I won't lie to you, Brooklyn. I won't do that just to get what I want, okay? I don't use manipulation."

"But you want me."

"I do. Quite a bit, actually. But we agreed not to kiss again, so I'm lying here, admitting what I want, knowing that it all hinges on one word from you. Because I never, ever want to treat you unfairly."

Her throat bobbed as she swallowed, and her eyes softened. "Even when you were trying to buy my house, you were always honest. I... I trust you, Cole."

The way she said it made him think that it was not something she admitted very often.

And then she surprised him by lifting up and shifting so that her mouth was against his.

He used gravity to his advantage, moving forward until she was back down on the sand, her head on his jacket, and he was braced above her, tasting her lips, which held the faint taste of vanilla and brown sugar from dessert. She was so sweet, so perfect. Her sweater was soft beneath his hand as he ran his hand up her arm and then behind her neck, cradling the soft skin and baby hairs there. She responded by nudging her left leg in between his, twining them together as he deepened the kiss. Her fingers gripped his arm as he slid his lips off hers and finally tasted the delectable hollow of her throat and she gasped, arching up. Without thinking, he ran his hand under her sweater to cup her breast in his palm, the pebbled tip pushing through her bra.

This was going far faster than he'd anticipated, and while his desire was yelling at him to take this as far as she'd let him, his caution—and conscience—told him to slow down. She wasn't his to ravish. She was his to protect.

And he had no freaking idea where that notion had come from, but it made him temper his advances, removing his hand from beneath her sweater and instead indulging in long, sweet kisses that drugged his mind.

At some point they slowed to gentle sips and nibbles, and then he pressed his forehead to hers. "Brooklyn. Please don't ask me to be sorry we did that. I'm not. No matter what happens, I'm not sorry."

She pushed away a bit. "What do you mean, whatever happens? Is there something I should know?"

Cole looked her fully in the eyes. "I don't live here. This house, this island, is part of my life but not all of it, not like it is yours. It's here for me to retreat to, for me to help others, too. Men and women like me, who forget to take care of themselves in their high-pressure lives."

"It's a piece of the puzzle that is Cole Abbott," she murmured.

"Exactly. And I like you and I want you…

but I don't want to build up expectations that aren't realistic."

"So this is a fling."

"No." He put his hand under her chin and lifted it. "Not a fling. You mean something to me, okay? Flings are…a couple of dates and some hot sex and not calling each other back. That's not us." It had been him, though. More times than he cared to admit.

And that alone scared him. The fact that he was saying all this out loud was terrifying. And yet he wanted to deal with her the way he ran his business—with integrity. She deserved it.

"But you'll be leaving."

"Yes, and soon."

She sighed, then sat up. Grains of sand clung to her sweater and he thought about the story she'd shared from her childhood. "Are you still close with your family, Brooklyn?"

She pulled up her knees and rested her arms on them, staring out at the dark ocean. "Not like I used to be. We're kind of spread out now."

But there was a hesitancy, a guardedness in her tone that made him curious. She could run her business anywhere. Why here, and why so isolated from everything? What was she running from?

He didn't have a chance to ask her as she jumped up from the sand and started brushing off her bottom. "You need to get back. You've left your guests a long time."

He gathered up his jacket, but then held out his hand. She paused, then took it, and they went back to where they'd abandoned their shoes. Once they'd brushed the sand off their feet and their footwear was back on, they took the narrow path toward Brooklyn's house.

The porch light was on, welcoming her back, and he fought against a sense of both wistfulness and homecoming. He was starting to realize how very much he'd wished to have someplace that felt like home and not just a dwelling…even if it was a dwelling he shared with other people. The closest he'd ever felt was Merrick, when he and Jeremy and Branson had been in boarding school together.

Back then it had been the people who had made it his home. But that wasn't true now. He'd only known Brooklyn a few weeks. He was at a loss to explain why the house felt so comfortable.

"I guess this is good-night," he said softly.

"Thank you for dinner. And for introducing me to your friends. They seem very, very nice."

"They are."

"And tell Raelynn her food was exquisite."

"All right."

He kissed her lightly this time, not pulling her close, but a gentle, slightly lingering contact that left his lips aching for more. But he'd do the smart thing and go home, have a whiskey with his pals and put this whole thing in perspective. Stars and moonlight did strange things to a man, didn't they?

"Good night," he said and stepped away.

"Good night. I'll wait to let Marvin out until after you're out of sight. Otherwise you won't get away for another twenty minutes."

He chuckled lightly, but his chest was tight at the feelings he was developing for this woman and her dog.

So he turned away and walked out of the circle of her porch light and back toward the mansion on the hill, waiting for him.

CHAPTER SEVEN

BROOKLYN WATCHED THE forecast carefully over the days ahead. The hurricane had been a category three as it barreled its way north, and now, maybe thirty-six hours away, had been downgraded to a cat two.

She made a trip to the mainland for supplies before the surf started picking up. Batteries, lamp oil, dog food and easy-to-prepare foods were top of her list. It wasn't her first storm, and she was fully prepared to spend a few evenings knitting by lantern light with a glass of wine if it came to that. There was still water in her rain barrels she could use for plumbing, and she filled two ten-gallon jugs that she'd use for drinking and cooking.

All models pointed to a direct hit just south of here as it made landfall, and even if it ended up as a category one, Brooklyn was pretty sure she'd lose power for several days. She had a small generator that would run her fridge and a few other things if required, but she relied on low-tech solutions to weather any outages.

She also hadn't heard from Cole since the night of the dinner party. She missed him. Of course, that in itself was a bad idea, so she didn't bother to initiate contact, either.

Instead she figured she'd have one lovely evening to remember; the night she stargazed with a billionaire and they made out on the beach. She smiled a little. It was a damned good memory, to be honest. One of those "there was this one time" stories. Had she really said she trusted him, and meant it?

Starlight was a funny, funny thing. Because for the first time in forever, she'd forgotten to feel threatened. Forgotten to be cautious.

She grabbed her lamps and filled them with lamp oil to shake away the unsettling thoughts. When the power went out, the darkness was the kind where a person couldn't see their hand in front of their face. Her favorite lighting was from the oil lamps. It was so warm and cozy. If she got cold, she'd put a fire on in the fireplace. She'd already brought wood into the back porch for that very reason.

Marvin sat by her feet. He'd been keeping rather close today, a good indication that storm weather was on its way. Outside it was sunny, but the air was still. Brooklyn was glad she'd gone over to the mainland and was already back. The surf would pick up soon, ahead of the storm. The wind would slip in, full of restless, restrained energy that shushed through the leaves. It was mild, too, the tropical air humid and heavy.

She wondered if Cole was prepared. His boat was still at the dock, and unless the helicopter had come while she was in town, he hadn't left the island.

Lamps filled and fresh batteries in her flashlights, she called Dan and then took Marvin and headed to the main house and garage. Marvin trotted ahead, and she called to him when they neared the garage where Dan and Raelynn lived. Dan met her in the drive, wearing a pair of rubber boots and a windbreaker.

"You're sure the tractor will tow his boat?"

She nodded. "Pretty sure. We only have to get them out of the water and to the boathouse. Then at least they won't smash up against the dock, and they'll be away from the trees."

Dan nodded and opened the garage door. "The key is in it. You're in charge, Brooklyn. I don't have a lot of experience with boats. Limos now...that's more my style."

"Don't worry. I know what to do. You just have to take orders." She grinned and winked at him, and he laughed. She liked Dan a lot. He and Raelynn made a really cute couple.

Brooklyn hopped up on the tractor and whistled for Marvin, who hopped up on the step beside her left foot. While Dan waited, she pressed in the clutch and brake and turned the key, the diesel engine rumbling to life. Marvin looked like she'd just given him the world's best present. He loved riding on the tractor. It was maybe bigger than required, but Ernest had always wanted the best. And she had to admit, in the winter, it did a heck of a job at snow removal once the blower attachment was installed.

They'd go to the boathouse and get the trailers, and then take the boats out of the water. Brooklyn wasn't taking any chances. Her boat was her only way on and off the island.

Cole went to his window when the strange rumbling sound touched his ears. To his amazement, he saw a big orange tractor heading down the lane, with Brooklyn in the driver's seat and Marvin's golden head beside her. Dan was walking behind, and Cole wondered what the heck they were up to.

More than that, he wondered why the sight of her driving a tractor made him so…curious. Her self-reliance never failed to impress him, but he hadn't imagined her using large machinery. She looked cute and incredibly capable.

That curiosity had his feet moving forward, stopping in the foyer for a light jacket. The storm was sending warm, moist air over the region, but he wasn't overly worried about any power outages. There was a huge generator wired in to his electrical panel, and he'd already told Raelynn and Dan to come to the main house if everything went dark.

Right now he wanted to know what Brooklyn was planning to do with that tractor.

When he started the downhill grade to her house, he saw exactly what she was doing. She and Dan had hooked a boat trailer to the tractor and right now Brooklyn was backing it to the water. The tide was in, so the ground held firm against the weight of the tires. Once the trailer was in the water, she locked the brake and hopped down, leaving the tractor running and giving Dan instructions.

Cole knew he should help, but he was fascinated watching her work.

She walked down the dock and unmoored her boat, guiding it expertly onto the trailer. When it was secured, she motioned to Dan to put the tractor in gear and pull them out. Dan released the brake and touched the throttle.

The tractor strained against the weight, but

bit by bit pulled the trailer forward until they were on the firm lane leading to the boat shed. Once they got there, she got the boat into the shed and unhooked the first trailer. Brooklyn swung the tractor around, backing it up to get the second trailer.

This time Cole approached, seeing as the second trailer was for his boat, and not her responsibility. Besides, he wanted to help. All his life this sort of thing had been for the "help" to do, but he wasn't above a little hands-on labor.

"Hello," he called out, and when Dan and Brooklyn turned around, he lifted a hand in a wave.

"Oh, hey!" Brooklyn called back to him, while Marvin heard his voice and made dizzying circles around Cole's legs.

"Marvin, take it easy, dude," Cole said, but laughed and gave the dog a good rub. "I see he also likes the tractor."

"We don't use it much in the summer. Unless a tree goes down or something, or we have to move the boats." She shoved her hands in her jacket pocket. "Ernest had a boat, too. Hence the two trailers."

"Well, let me help this time, since it's my boat."

"Sure. Dan's got his boots on. I'll back up

the tractor, you can pilot it in, and Dan can help secure it. Easy-peasy."

Marvin hopped back up in his spot of honor and they worked as a team. It took no time at all to get the boat on the trailer. The boat was heavier than hers, though, and took a little more work on the part of the tractor to get it up top to the shed. To Cole's surprise, she backed the trailer in expertly, so both boats were protected from the elements.

To say he was impressed was an understatement.

Together they shut the boathouse doors and she killed the tractor engine. "Would you two like a cup of coffee or something?"

Dan looked like he wanted to say yes, but reluctantly shook his head. "I told Raelynn I'd be back up to do some hurricane prep. We still have to move the patio furniture and stuff inside."

Cole appreciated it but didn't want to begrudge the guy a simple drink. "There's time, Dan. No need to rush back."

"Seriously," Brooklyn said, "a pot takes five minutes to brew. And because you both helped, the boat thing went pretty fast."

"All right then. If you do, Cole."

"Sure."

Cole watched as Dan chatted to Brooklyn

and Marvin trotted behind them. Dan was a friendly guy and so easygoing. He and Brooklyn were relaxed, like old friends. He thought back to his dinner party and how sometimes Brooklyn looked a little awkward or uncomfortable. He wasn't usually so aware of their differences in lifestyle, but watching her drive the tractor and laughing with Dan, he realized that in many ways they were as different as the sun and moon.

"Cole, you coming?" she called back.

"Yep. Be right there."

Marvin stood before him, tennis ball in his mouth. The moment Cole made eye contact with the dog, the tennis ball was dropped at his feet. Cole chuckled and picked it up, then threw it into the grass. He did this twice before Brooklyn came back, a cup of coffee in her hands. "Here, stop playing with the dog and have a coffee."

He smiled up at her. "But he asked so nicely."

She snorted. "He always does."

He went to take the mug from her and their fingers touched. The contact sparked a memory of that night under the stars, and how they'd touched each other, gently and carefully, and he knew staying was the wrong move. But he couldn't leave now, not with Dan coming out onto the front porch with his own cup. Cole would have to remain polite and no more. Otherwise he was going to find himself in a place he couldn't get out of.

They all sat on the front porch and sipped their coffee, talking about the forecast and what they might expect. None of them were strangers to hurricanes; the storms often made their way up the East Coast. But this was the first time Cole would be on a tiny island in the ocean and not comfortable in the family mansion or an elite boarding school. Maybe they weren't far from the mainland, but once the storm came in, there would be no getting off the island until it passed. It was a different sort of feeling, being at the mercy of Mother Nature.

"The storm's still a cat two," Dan said. "That'll cause some serious damage."

"And depending on when it hits, the storm surge could really be devastating." Brooklyn frowned. "Cole, is your friend Branson ready? His place is lovely, but so close to the shore. The cliffs aren't very high, either."

"You know it?"

She smiled. "Everyone knows that property. The lighthouse was a legendary make-out spot in high school."

Dan laughed and Cole was left wondering if she'd ever gone to the lighthouse for that sort of activity. But he wasn't going to ask. He didn't need that picture in his brain if she confirmed it.

"I hope so. Jeremy, too. We're all right in the path."

Silence fell for a few moments, and he noticed the wind had an eerie sound to it. "It feels weird."

Brooklyn smiled a little. "The wind? Yeah. The waves are gonna pick up really soon. By tomorrow night we'll be in the thick of it. But you wait. Before it hits? There'll be tons of surfers out catching the swell." She shook her head. "That's not for me. Last time we had a storm this big, power was out on the mainland for five days. I guess I'm chill about it once I'm prepared, but I don't see it as something to play with."

Cole looked over at her and saw lines of worry near her eyes. "You know if it looks bad, you can come out to the house and wait it out with us. Marvin, too."

"Oh, we'll be fine. Not our first rodeo."

He knew she would be. She was one of the most independent, capable women he'd ever met. "Of course you will. But you're welcome just the same."

"Thank you."

He downed what was left in his cup and

stood. "Well, thanks for the coffee, but I should probably be getting back. I've been working with the New York office today, and I have a call at four that I need to prep for."

"I'll head back with you, and take the tractor," Dan agreed. "But you can ride shotgun if you want to, boss."

Brooklyn laughed and snorted, and Cole couldn't stop the smile that spread over his face. She was so darned artless.

"I'll walk. And see you there." He met Brooklyn's gaze. "Thank you for moving my boat. Please be careful during the storm, okay?"

Her smile slipped and she nodded. "I will. You do the same. And we can check in when it's over."

"The invitation still stands. You and Marvin are welcome any time."

She nodded.

He tried not to think about her down here all alone if things got scary. She was a big girl and could take care of herself.

But damned if he didn't want to. Why did he keep having that impulse?

CHAPTER EIGHT

HURRICANE PAULA ROARED into Nova Scotia as a strong category one. Before it ever made official landfall, power was out all over the south shore. Brooklyn stared out the window at the wind and rain. It wasn't raining heavily yet; this was just one of the outer bands getting started. But this was gearing up to be a doozy, and for the first time ever she was nervous about being here at the house.

It was only four o'clock and still daylight, but soon darkness would fall as the worst of the storm wreaked havoc on her island. Marvin sat at her knee, never moving. He was a loyal companion, always at her side at any sign of trouble. She patted his head and rubbed his ears. And thought of Cole and Dan and Raelynn, up at the house, hopefully safe and cozy.

There was a large crack and a whoosh and she jumped up and ran to the window. One of the trees in her front yard had broken off, tilting awkwardly into the lane. She looked down at Marvin again. The sound had startled him and now he was panting. Good heavens, this was just the prelude. And as much as she loved the little house, she realized she really didn't want to be alone right now. Not when there was company to be had.

"Come on, Marvin." She went to grab his leash and filled a zipped baggie with kibble. Then she took her waterproof pack and put the kibble and a change of clothes inside, along with her toothbrush. There were three people at the house and he had extended the offer, after all. Things would be fine until morning, and then she'd come down and run the generator as cleanup began.

She pulled on her raincoat and boots, fastening the hood of her jacket around her chin with the Velcro closing. With Marvin's leash tight in her hand, she locked the door with the other hand and tested it, then kept her eye on the handful of trees nearby, just in case they too succumbed to the wind. A gust buffeted her and she staggered, but then she gripped the leash and started toward the other end of the island. Marvin squinted against the driving rain but trotted along beside her.

To her right she could see the coastline,

and the wild spray that filled the air as the big waves crashed onto the rocks.

Paula was far more dangerous than her name sounded.

By the time they got to Cole's, Marvin was soaking wet and she was breathless from fighting the wind. She knocked on the front door, suddenly wondering if this was an awful idea. Marvin was going to be wet and probably make a mess; she'd be dripping everywhere. A nasty gust of wind slammed into them both and she hunched forward. What if he hadn't heard her knock?

She just raised her hand to knock again when the door opened, and Cole stood there in the breach. His mouth was open in surprise as he took in what she was sure had to be a bedraggled sight—one woman in a canary yellow raincoat and a very wet dog with his tail not quite between his legs, but definitely in a displeased position. Another gust of wind sent a wash of rain over them and partly into Cole's foyer. "You'd better come in, before you blow away."

She stepped inside and let him close the door, but didn't move inside. "I'm soaking wet, I'm afraid. And going to drip over your foyer."

"That's what towels are for. Hang on."

He disappeared for a moment, then came

back with two fluffy towels. He took Marvin's leash while she removed her raincoat and boots, and then used a towel to blot her face and arms. She was just about to reach for Marvin when he started an all-over body shudder and shook, spraying water all over the foyer and Cole's clean pants.

"Oh, Marvin!" Brooklyn let out a huge sigh. "I'm sorry, Cole. What a mess."

Again, he laughed. "It's water. It won't hurt anything." He took Marvin's towel and started rubbing it over the dog's back and down his legs. "Yeah, you like that, don't you?" Marvin wore a blissful doggy expression and Brooklyn rolled her eyes. That creature loved anything to do with pats, scratches or rubs. He didn't even mind when Cole lifted his feet and dried off each pad.

"Is it okay that we're here? With the power out and all, and then a tree came down in front of the house, and I just thought…"

"You thought what?" He stood, holding the towel in his hands, watching her intently.

Heat rushed into her cheeks. "The worst of the storm is set to be after dark. It just felt… a little lonely. I mean, there are lots of times when I've weathered storms alone because there's no one here. But you are here, and Rae-lynn and Dan, and—"

"You don't have to explain. I told you that you were welcome to join us and I meant it. There's lots of room, we've got power thanks to the generator, and we'll be cozy as anything."

"I'll try to make sure Marvin behaves himself."

In response, Cole reached down and unclipped Marvin's leash. "Don't be silly. He's a great dog. Come on, Marvin. Let's get a treat."

At the word "treat," the dog's ears perked up and he followed closely on Cole's heels as Cole started down the hall toward the kitchen.

"He doesn't really eat people food," she cautioned. The last thing she needed was for Marvin to have some sort of gastro episode in the middle of the storm.

"How about some cheese? Or some carrots?"

Brooklyn followed the duo into the kitchen. "I suppose a little would be all right. I did bring kibble with me."

"Perfect. Let me find a bowl for water."

He dug around in the cupboards until he found a stainless steel mixing bowl, which he filled with water and put on the floor. Then he went into the fridge and grabbed a platter. It contained cubed cheese, meats and had a bunch of green grapes in the center. "Hungry?"

She'd eaten lunch but it had been a simple grilled cheese. "I wouldn't mind a few grapes."

"Great. Make yourself at home." He took three cubes of cheese and went over to Marvin. "Marvin, sit."

Marvin's butt hit the tile floor.

Cole turned to Brooklyn with a wide smile that made him look ridiculously boyish. "I didn't think he'd really do it."

"Ask him to shake a paw, and offer your non-cheese hand."

He turned back, leaned over. "Marvin, shake a paw." He held out his hand, and Marvin lifted his paw and placed it on Cole's palm.

"Good boy! Have a piece of cheese." Cole fed him the cube of cheddar. Marvin took it delicately, and once more Brooklyn marveled at the wide smile on Cole's face. He really did love dogs. It was a crying shame that he was in his thirties and had never had one. Marvin added so much to her life.

"There's a fire on in the fireplace. Why don't you bring your grapes and come in? Do you want a coffee? Brandy or cognac?"

She'd forgotten that she was moving into the lap of luxury by coming to Cole's. "I wouldn't say no to coffee, but show me where the stuff is. I can make it. You don't have to wait on me."

"Don't be silly. I know how to run a coffee maker."

He did, too. Before long there were two steaming mugs. He even steamed milk for hers and poured the froth in, making a rich, aromatic latte. "See?"

She wasn't used to fancy coffee. But she certainly wasn't going to say no. "Thanks. That smells great."

She followed him to the living room. Even though the storm raged outside, and she could see it through the windows, there was warm light from a tall lamp and the flicker of the gas fireplace. It threw some heat and Brooklyn picked a chair near the fire, settling into it with a sigh. It was so incredibly comfortable she nearly sighed again. Cole sat on the sofa opposite her and lifted his mug to taste his coffee.

Marvin went up to the fireplace, stared at the flames for a moment, and then turned around twice before flopping down in front of it.

Brooklyn laughed and looked over at Cole. "That's it. He's made himself at home for the duration."

"Good," Cole decreed. "And how about you?"

She smiled faintly. Cole looked delectable in his slightly damp trousers and thick-knit sweater. "I'm getting there. But I feel a little odd being here. It's a gorgeous house, Cole. I keep feeling I'll break something expensive."

"Don't worry about that. I'll buy another." He flashed her his grin and she smiled in return, but only for a moment.

"Yes, but you see, that just highlights how different our lives are."

He shrugged. "Does it matter? I mean, it's only money."

She stared down in her cup for a moment before looking up and meeting his gaze again. "The people who generally say that are the ones who have lots of it," she countered. "At one point, my family owned this whole island. They had to sell most of it for financial reasons. For a lot of people, money means freedom. Freedom to choose what sort of life they'll have. The less money, the more limited the choices."

"I realize that." His voice had softened. "I just meant that I want you to be comfortable and not worry about how much something here costs."

"I know that. It just…got my hackles up a bit." She gave a little laugh. "Pride. I still have some, apparently."

"You sure do." He drank more of his coffee. "Why don't you sit over here with me? The heat from the fire will still reach you, and it feels weird talking to you way over there."

The room was very large and it did seem as if there was a lot of space between them. She probably shouldn't, but she got up and moved over to the sofa, sitting at the other end and tucking her feet up beneath her. "Better?"

"Much." His soft eyes met hers. "I'm very glad you're here, Brooklyn."

A gust of wind rattled the window and they both looked over. The window was streaked with rain and the beach grasses were waving furiously.

"It seems so strange being inside with power while that's going on out there," she remarked.

"Ernest was smart and had the generator wired in. With only two houses on the island, I'm guessing it'd be the last on the list to have power restored. You could go days without it here."

She nodded. "One time when I was small, we got caught in a nor'easter in January. No generators on the island back then. We cooked on my grandmother's woodstove and used oil lamps for light." She smiled fondly at the memory. "We melted snow for water and we did puzzles and played cards. Good memories."

"It sounds perfect," Cole said, and she noticed his smile wasn't quite as immediate as before.

"Did I say something wrong?"

"Oh, no, of course not. I'm just finding that every time you share a memory, I envy you your childhood a little more."

"Yours was lonely. But then you met Branson and Jeremy."

He nodded. "Yes, I did. And they saved me. Anything I learned about affection and loyalty and friendship, I learned from them."

It sounded awfully sad just the same.

"I think we're opposites," she replied softly. "My family gave lots of love and support. But it's the real world that's let me down."

"How so?"

She hesitated, and he must have sensed her discomfort, because he said, "Never mind. If you're not comfortable talking about it, we won't."

It was a moment in which she could choose to trust him or not. They'd become friends, but she wasn't yet sure what sort of friends. They'd made out on the beach and it had been glorious. But since then he'd been perfectly platonic, as she'd asked.

She liked that about him. Even as she thought about kissing him again, she liked that she'd set a boundary and he'd accepted it without question. She liked it a lot.

Marvin got up from the spot in front of the fire and came to her side. He sat and put his head on her knee, and her heart softened. "Marvin is not a trained therapy dog, but you'd think he was. He's my best friend in the world."

Cole's gaze was steady. "If you don't want to answer this, I'll respect it. Is there a reason why you'd need a therapy dog?"

Brooklyn swallowed around the large lump in her throat. It had been a few years now, and it wasn't exactly a secret. After all, it had been on the news and the communities in this part of the province were small. But choosing to tell someone was different.

Because it was telling, and not just having them know.

Cole slid over on the sofa and took her hand in his. His hand was warm, in contrast to her cold one. He chafed it a bit and said gently, "You don't have to tell me if you don't want to. The last thing I want is to upset you."

She looked up at him. "Are you even real?"

"What do you mean?"

"I mean you're rich and you look like...that, and it's crazy that you're this nice as well. I keep wondering where your flaws are."

"Oh," he said darkly, "I have them. Never fear."

She sighed as he twined his fingers with hers. Marvin still pressed close to her knees, and she felt very comforted and protected in that moment. Something that was in short supply most of the time, even though she faked bravery whenever she was out of her comfort zone.

"It happened a few years ago, in town, in the middle of the afternoon."

Cole held on to Brooklyn's hand firmly, waiting for her to go on. She'd paused, and he would be patient, because he sensed what she was going to say was important. And it was unusual and flattering that she trusted him with whatever her story was. Not many people did. Only two, really. Jeremy and Branson. The truth was that other than his best buddies, Cole didn't have close relationships. And fears? He hadn't lied. He was 100 percent a commitment-phobe and, despite seeing it in his best friends, wasn't sure he really believed in love, either.

But he liked Brooklyn, more than any woman he'd ever met. There was something so real about her. He never questioned her motives. She was unfailingly honest and authentic, with no hidden agenda.

And right now, a wild storm was raging outside and she was holding onto his hand for dear life. He knew he should be cautious. That he should not want to get involved in whatever personal things she had going on. But she was also letting him in, and there was something addictive about knowing someone trusted you enough to share a secret. It wasn't something that he was used to. It was also something he usually avoided, but with Brooklyn, it felt oddly safe.

He rubbed his thumb over her hand, encouraging her to go on.

"I was home for the weekend, and I went into the liquor store to buy a bottle of wine for my mom and me. We were going to have a wine and movie night, because I was heading into finals and needed some downtime to chill.

"So I'm waiting in line with my wine, and this guy comes in. I didn't think anything about it. I barely even noticed him. And then he walks up to the cashier in front of me and pulls a gun out of his jacket."

"My God," Cole exclaimed. "In a town that small? Does that sort of thing happen often? I mean, I kind of pictured a crime rate of about zero."

"Bad things happen everywhere," she whispered.

"I'm sorry. Go on."

She hesitated and he waited. Not that he wanted to pressure her, but he got the feeling she needed to say it. Marvin let out a whine and nudged her leg, and she reached down with her other hand and patted his head. "Thanks, Marv," she murmured. "Okay." Her voice strengthened. "We all did exactly what he said. We didn't move. The cashiers gave him the money. But they'd also hit the panic button, and once he had the money he started to freak out. So he grabbed me and dragged me outside with him."

Cole swore. She'd been part of an armed robbery. No wonder she was skittish.

"His car was outside. I'd dropped my bottle of wine and it broke everywhere, and I had a piece of glass in the top of my foot. He opened the driver's side and shoved me in, and then got in after me. There was a split second where I froze, but then I remembered watching a show and hearing that the one thing you should never do is go to a second location with someone, so I unlocked the door and jumped out, hoping he wouldn't use the gun. He didn't. He took off, and I was left there on the sidewalk."

She was trembling now, so he slid closer and enfolded her in his arms. "You're safe now," he said gently and kissed her hair. His heart hurt for her. What a terrifying ordeal. "You were smart and did everything right."

"That's what the cops said. I was able to give

a good description and a partial plate. He was arrested shortly after."

"So you got Marvin."

"Not at first. I went through all the victim services stuff, and some counseling, but I really struggled. I left school, which I still regret sometimes. Eventually I got Marvin, and then I came over to the island for a few days to get away. It was the first time I'd felt peace in months, so I asked if I could move over here for a while. Two years and counting and I'm still here. My grandmother deeded me the property so it would be in the family but she wouldn't have to deal with it. Marvin's been with me through all of that."

Cole held her close but was gratified to see that she'd stopped shaking. "He's quite a dog," he said. "And you're quite a woman."

"I ran away. That's not so remarkable. Heck, I still fight a lot of panic when I go into town. Waiting in line anywhere is torture. And I have a handful of places I like to go and that's it. I'm still horribly afraid."

"You also live on this island by yourself, run your own business and are as competent a person as I've ever met. Maybe certain situations trigger you, but I promise you, they don't define who you are. The way you stood up to me when I arrived..."

She laughed, a sound thick with emotion. "Oh, Cole. I thought I was going to throw up the whole time. But this place means so much to me. There was no way I was going to give it up without a fight."

He thought for a moment, then turned a bit and made her face him. "You listen to me," he said. "You are brave. Being brave doesn't mean not being afraid. It means being afraid and doing it anyway. There is nothing I respect more, Brooklyn. And I'm honored that you shared it with me." Honored and a bit terrified, but he'd work through that.

She looked down and bit her lip. He didn't want to make her cry, but couldn't she see how remarkable she was? "What were you taking in school?"

"Chemistry. I was trying to get into the pharmacy program."

He grinned. "Smarty-pants."

She finally smiled. "Whatever."

The wind howled around the windows and Cole realized that at some point it had gotten dark outside. "Looks like we're stormed in for sure, now," he commented. "I'm glad you came. I'm glad that my house is a place you feel safe."

She turned her liquid eyes to his and said simply, "You love my dog. That's my first litmus test."

Did he? Did he love Marvin? He looked down at the yellow fur and big brown eyes and realized he did, in fact, love this dog. He was friendship and loyalty and love all wrapped up in one four-legged package. He was the friend that Cole had wanted his whole life, and Cole was even more glad that Brooklyn had him to keep her from being lonely. Maybe moving to the island had been an extreme reaction on her part, but she'd been through something rather extreme. Who was he to judge?

After all, he wasn't the king of perfect life choices, was he?

"Rae and Dan will be coming over soon for dinner. You don't mind, do you?"

Her face brightened. "No, not at all! I like them both, very much. It was one of the reasons I came up here today. I kind of liked the thought of, well, everyone together."

"Me, too," he said, and realized it was true. Raelynn and Dan were employees, but they were more than that to Cole.

"Hey, Cole?"

He looked into her face. Her tears had dried, but her eyes remained that steady, piercing blue that had reached in and grabbed him from day one, when he'd expected an old lady and was met with her instead.

"Thank you for listening. And for letting go of the idea of buying me out. It means a lot."

"You're welcome," he said, unsure of what else to say. He had never agreed to let go of his desire to purchase her property, but now that she'd said it, he knew he could not pressure her to sell and take away her safe place. Even if it was a place to hide.

Everyone had a right to hide if they wanted to. He looked around the huge living room. Even him.

CHAPTER NINE

THE RAIN SLASHED and the windows rattled, but Cole's kitchen was the port in the storm for the four occupants of the island. Brooklyn looked around and felt a warmth that had eluded her for a long, long time. These people felt like her friends. The class difference didn't seem to matter, even though Brooklyn was always aware of the opulence around her.

Cole had spared no expense in updating the house, and she'd caught a glimpse of his sweater tag before dinner. She was pretty sure that it cost as much as most of her wardrobe put together. The towel he'd given her earlier had been of the finest, plushiest cotton. Cole Abbott was a man used to the best.

But he was also a lot more fun than she'd imagined.

The four of them had eaten a delicious meal of carbonara and salad that Raelynn had prepared, eating in the kitchen rather than the formal dining room. Once the mess was cleaned up, Cole had opened up another bottle of wine and suggested they play cards. Brooklyn wondered if he'd done that because of what she'd said earlier, and making her want to feel at home. Either way, the result was that they were now sitting around the kitchen table. Rae, as she asked Brooklyn to call her, and Brooklyn had glasses of Shiraz at their elbows, while the men had switched to scotch.

The game they all agreed on was hearts, and so far Dan was trouncing everyone. He never seemed to end up with the queen of spades, and as the evening progressed, the storm howled and shook the house, and Raelynn topped up their glasses once more, Brooklyn couldn't remember a time when she'd had so much fun.

Cole's eyes were the color of cornflowers as they twinkled at her over his cards, and she grinned back. The smile playing on his lips was mesmerizing, and she found herself staring at his mouth for too long as she remembered kissing him on the beach.

"Your turn," Raelynn said, and Brooklyn dragged her gaze away and back to the cards in her hand.

This was the one hand where she couldn't pass three cards to anyone. She was stuck with what she had, and she was getting tired of always ending up with a mitt full of hearts counting against her. She also had the two of clubs, so she started the hand and placed each card carefully. One after the other she ended up with hearts, and the other three were teasing her about how badly she was playing. But in the end, she played the queen of spades and reveled in the shock on their faces when they all realized she'd taken every single heart and the queen, too.

Which meant she had no penalty and they all had to count the points against themselves.

"Oh, that was sneaky!" Dan exclaimed, pointing his finger at her. "Damn you, Brookie!"

She burst out laughing. "Brookie? No one has called me that since I was nine!"

Raelynn joined in, and Cole raised an eyebrow. "Brookie," he said, his smooth voice teasing.

"Don't even think about it," she warned, leveling him with a glare.

He grinned and sat back in his chair. "Deal again. I need to redeem myself."

At some point they switched to playing rummy and Raelynn got up to make popcorn. Finally, about midnight, Raelynn and Dan decided to call it a night.

"You're sure you don't want to stay here?"

Cole asked, frowning. The apartment over the garage wasn't powered by the generator, so they'd be going to a dark home.

"We've got flashlights and blankets." Rae winked at him. "Don't you worry about us. We won't get cold."

Brooklyn snorted and that set everyone laughing again. The pair bundled up in rain-coats and headed out into the storm to make the short trek to their apartment.

"I had fun," Brooklyn said. Her brain was a little fuzzy from the wine, but the evening had been long and there'd been more sipping than drinking. It was a pleasant, warm feel-ing brought on by the excellent shiraz and the company.

"Me, too," Cole said. "Way more than I usu-ally do. Cutthroat hearts was so much better than gallery openings and charity benefits."

"Oh, that sounds dull as dirt," she remarked.

"It is, most of the time." He leaned against the kitchen counter and tilted his head as he studied her. "Is this what normal people do on a Saturday night?"

"Around here? As often as not. Maybe a movie. Or watching the hockey game on TV."

"That sounds heavenly."

"Oh, be serious."

He pushed away from the counter and came

to her. She was in the midst of picking up dirty glasses from the table and he stayed her motions with a hand on her wrist. "No, I mean it, Brooklyn. I'm so glad you came here tonight. You have this talent for making people at home no matter where you are."

Heat rushed into her face, both from the praise and from the intimate touch on her arm. "Thank you," she said, working hard to accept the compliment and not brush it off. He was being earnest, and she respected that.

And his gaze dropped from her eyes to her lips and clung there, while her pulse leaped and her breath quickened. They shouldn't kiss again. It would muddy the waters. And yet… she wanted to. Tonight their relationship had changed. They were no longer casual acquaintances. She'd shared something personal with him, and he'd invited her into his home. They'd laughed together. Trash-talked over cards. They were real friends now.

Friends who apparently also had this buzz of attraction humming between them.

She was the one who made the first move. It only took a step for her to be a breath away from him. She held a wineglass in each hand and was glad of it, or else she might have put her arms around his neck and drawn him close. But she did lift her chin, a silent invitation, and met his gaze evenly. Cole Abbott surprised her, and in the nicest way. Maybe this would complicate things. But she'd had enough shiraz to lose a bit of caution where Cole was concerned.

"Brooklyn," he murmured. "Be sure."

And still she held his gaze, even though inside she was trembling.

He leaned forward. It didn't take much, and his lips touched hers. At the first contact her eyelids fluttered closed, and she focused on the feel of his lips. How could they be firm and yet so soft at the same time? He tasted slightly of the scotch from earlier, warm and mellow and expensive. His hand curled around the nape of her neck and his fingertips rubbed the tight tendons there, so perfectly that she nearly moaned with pleasure.

But she wouldn't. Because kissing was one thing, but losing control was another, and she was not going to lose control. Not tonight. This felt too fragile. Too…new. Different even from their interlude on the beach—deeper somehow.

"You taste good," he murmured, nipping at her lips.

"So do you."

They kissed a while longer, not rushing, until there was a whine at her feet.

Marvin sat there looking up at them, an anxious look in his eyes.

Brooklyn took the opportunity to step back and clear her head from the seductive haze that was Cole. "Well, hello, sleepyhead." Marvin had curled up in front of the fire and snoozed most of the evening. "I suppose you need to go outside."

Cole took the crystal glasses from her hands. "I'll deal with these. You take him outside. Or if you want, we can go out together. It's not as bad as it was, but it's still a storm and it's pitch-black outside."

"My things are by the front door," she said, patting her leg for Marvin to follow. "But I wouldn't say no to the company."

Brooklyn headed to the front door, but instead of his usual trot, Marvin plodded along behind her. "You can't still be sleepy," she chided him, reaching for her raincoat. "You've been a lazybones all night."

He looked up at her and whined again. Maybe it was the storm, she reasoned. Marvin wasn't himself, but they were in a strange house with the remnants of a hurricane blustering outside.

"What's wrong?" Cole joined her a moment later, shrugging on a jacket.

"Marvin's slow. And whining a bit. Hopefully he's not scared."

Cole handed her a flashlight. "Here. We should have a light."

Together they opened the door and went outside. Marvin hesitated in the doorway, but then went down the few steps to the path and found a nearby bush to pee on. He started to trot away, so Brooklyn and Cole followed, the flashlight beam illuminating the rain that seemed to be falling sideways in the brisk wind.

But it was definitely not as bad as earlier. The worst was probably over now.

Marvin hunched over and Brooklyn followed with a poop bag; she wasn't about to leave his mess on Cole's lawn. But when she went to him, she saw him straining with very little progress. And then when he did have success, there was blood.

Her heart froze a little. His uncharacteristic lethargy, the whining, the blood…something was wrong with Marvin. And they were stuck on this island with no power, and no way off. Even if the storm eased, the sea was too wild for either of their boats.

"Cole?" She called through the wind, and he ran over to her right away. Had her voice sounded as panicked as she felt? "There's something wrong with Marvin. There's blood, and…" Her throat closed over.

Cole took the flashlight. Marvin was whining, loud enough they could hear him over the wind, and tears of fear stung her eyes. "Marv, what is it, huh? You not feeling good, buddy?"

"Let's get him inside."

She nodded, and they urged the dog to follow them back to the house. She toweled him off carefully, trying to stay calm. "There you go, sweetie. All dry." She looked at Cole. "Let's see if he'll drink."

They went back into the kitchen, and then Brooklyn realized that Marvin hadn't eaten the kibble she'd put out at supper time. She'd had a fine time, eating and drinking and laughing and kissing Cole...and her best friend had been getting sick.

"He didn't eat," she whispered.

The dog sniffed the bowl of food, looked at the water and turned away.

"Okay," Cole said, taking her hands. "Who's your vet?"

"Dr. Thorpe in Liverpool. But he's unlikely to have power..."

"Does he have a cell number?"

She nodded. "He gave it to me once when Marvin was a puppy and we had an emergency. I think it's still in my phone..."

Cole squeezed her fingers. "Okay. I know it's late, but call him. See if he has power."

Tears slipped down her cheeks. "Even if he does, we can't get off the island. Not with the swell being what it is."

"First things first. You call. I'm going to check into some things." He paused and kissed her forehead. "Marvin's going to be okay, Brooklyn."

She sniffed and pulled her hands away. "Okay. I'm going to look for the number."

Cole slipped away and went to another room, and Brooklyn retrieved her phone. With shaking fingers, she scrolled through her contacts until she found Dr. Thorpe's number. He didn't answer for the first four rings, but on the fifth he picked up, and she let out a breath, determined not to cry or panic.

As they were talking, Marvin started to throw up. There was only bile, which she relayed to the vet as calmly as she could, as well as Marvin's other symptoms. With a promise to call him back with any updates or an estimated time of arrival, she clicked off the call, started crying again and went searching for something to clean up after Marvin.

Cole came back and found her on the floor, a contrite and subdued Marvin beside her. "Did you reach him?"

She nodded and balled up the paper towel she'd found under the sink. "I'm to watch him for worsening symptoms and call him immediately if he gets worse or if we manage to get to the mainland." She looked up at Cole, her eyes wet. "There's no way. Even if we could handle the waves, the boats are locked away and we'd have to get them out of the boat shed and launch them..."

She got up and went to the garbage can, then washed her hands. "Oh, Cole, I'm so sorry this has happened when you've been so kind."

"Don't be silly. You haven't done anything wrong." Marvin was now lying on the kitchen floor and she saw the worry crease Cole's forehead. "I made a few calls. If we can hold out another few hours, I might have a way for us to get him to the vet."

She stared at him. "How?"

"My helicopter pilot. We have the pad here. He's monitoring the winds and will call me the moment he's cool with taking off." He came forward and cupped her face in his hands. "It won't be a fun flight, but it'll be short. You just have to hang on a little longer."

She nodded, incredibly touched amid all the worry tangling in her stomach.

Then watched as Cole, in his thousand-dollar sweater, knelt down gently, picked up all eighty pounds of her sick dog in his arms and went toward the living room. She followed him, swallowing sobs at the caring and loving way he was handling her beloved pet. And in the living room, instead of putting him on the rug in front of the fire, Cole put Marvin down on the sofa and sat down beside him. "There you are, dude," he said soothingly, and Brooklyn sat down on the other side of Marvin.

"Cole, your sofa...he might be sick again. Or...worse."

Cole met her gaze. "So what? It's just a sofa. He needs to be comfortable and loved. And you need to be beside him."

She had no idea how to answer, so she simply stroked Marvin's head and prayed he'd be okay, and that this was some weird thing and he wasn't very ill at all.

Cole and Brooklyn sat with Marvin into the night. Though Cole tried feeding him by hand and offering him water, the dog wouldn't eat or drink. He threw up again, but Cole had retrieved the towel from earlier and put it nearby. It saved the sofa and towels were easily replaced.

Dogs weren't. Even though Cole had never had such a companion, all he needed to do was see the look of anguish on Brooklyn's face to know that Marvin had to be okay. Cole would do anything in his power to ensure it. Even wake his pilot and have a chopper chartered in the tail end of a hurricane.

Besides, he was horribly fond of Marvin himself. Other than his two best friends, he'd never received such an enthusiastic greeting as he did when he entered Brooklyn's yard and Marvin came running out to meet him, barking and with a wildly wagging tail.

His cell rang and he jumped, then answered it. The call was brief, and then he clicked off and met Brooklyn's hopeful gaze.

"He'll be here in about an hour. It'd be faster, but he's got to deal with the wind. Call the vet and give him the heads-up. You're sure he has power?"

"The clinic is also on a generator. I'll call him."

"I'm arranging for a car to meet us at the airstrip."

"Cole, I don't know what to say." Her eyes were luminous with tears and gratitude. "This is… I can't even tell you."

"Hush. Make your call and I'll make sure we're ready to go."

It took some doing to get a car service, and a promise of a very nice monetary incentive. He also called Dan, updating him on the situation and letting him know there'd be a helicopter landing shortly. He wasn't surprised when Dan and Raelynn showed up ten minutes later, concern etched on their faces. They weren't just employees, they were wonderful people and Brooklyn had won them over, too.

Too. There was no denying that he was more involved with her than he ever intended. That kiss in the kitchen tonight had been soft and sweet and so different from anything he'd ever experienced. For a guy who didn't do intimacy, he was up to his neck in it right now.

Raelynn had made tea and pushed a cup in Brooklyn's hands. "Here. Drink some of this and breathe."

It was good advice, but everyone was on edge. Marvin had gotten down from the sofa, but he was so devoid of his usual energy. He once again sniffed at the bowls but turned away. He whined pitifully and then lay down on the floor, resting on his side.

Cole saw Brooklyn's face start to crumple again, so he went to her and squeezed her shoulder.

Moments later they heard the rhythmic *whomp-whomp* of the helicopter approaching. Cole shrugged on his jacket, then held out Brooklyn's so she could slip her arms in. When Dan gave the go-ahead, he once again hefted Marvin into his arms—the dead weight made him stagger slightly—and headed toward the helipad.

Brooklyn jogged beside him, carrying a blanket that Raelynn had pressed into her hands.

"Hang on tight," the pilot shouted over the noise, but his face wore a grin. "Fasten your seat belts. It'll be bumpy but short."

Brooklyn's face was pale and he wondered if she was afraid of the helicopter or for Marvin. She'd mentioned going on a ride with Ernest once, but that wasn't in the dark in nasty weather, either. He patted her hand and gave her a headset. Then he put on his own.

"Don't worry," he said into the mic. "Dave's a former navy pilot. He's used to landing on a pitching deck. Dry land is a breeze, right Dave?"

"Yes, sir," Dave answered. "Ready?"

It was not an easy trip, even though it was, as Dave promised, a short one. Wind buffeted the aircraft and more than once Cole's stomach did a hollow flip. Brooklyn's fingers were tight in Marvin's fur, and Cole's brow wrinkled in concern as Marvin panted heavily. Was it the stress of the ride, or his illness? Thankfully, they weren't in the air very long, and were soon nearing the tiny Liverpool airport. Dave set the chopper down expertly and promised to stay nearby for the return trip whenever Cole required it.

For the third time, Cole lifted Marvin—still bundled in the blanket—out of the helicopter and to the waiting cab he'd convinced to pick them up.

The cabbie lifted an eyebrow at the sight of the dog but said nothing about it as he opened the back door for them. "Dr. Thorpe's vet clinic," Cole said as Brooklyn crawled in the other side. He realized that the dog had always been sandwiched between the two of them since he'd started getting sick.

"Have to take the long way. One of the roads is flooded. Heck of a storm," the cabbie said.

"Whatever gets us there fast and safe," Cole replied.

The sun wasn't yet up, and power was out, making everything eerily dark. The headlights illuminated a narrow swath, but enough that Cole could see downed branches and a few trees snapped off. Lights were on at a square building, though, with a parking lot out front. "Looks like the doc has a generator running," the driver said, pulling in. "Lucky for you, eh?"

"Very." Brooklyn leaned forward toward the front seat. "Thank you so much for coming out to get us. It means a lot."

"Oh, no problem."

Cole knew it was no problem because he'd paid handsomely for the service. But he admired Brooklyn's kindness and courtesy. She appreciated people, and he liked that about her.

Dr. Thorpe came out and met them at the door, and for the first time, Cole didn't have to lift Marvin. Cole was in good shape, but eighty pounds of deadweight dog was a challenge. He and Brooklyn followed the vet into the building and then into an exam room. Cole stood back while Brooklyn relayed Marvin's symptoms, and then the two of them went to the waiting room while Dr. Thorpe and his assistant, who Cole quickly learned was his wife, did the examination.

He looked over at Brooklyn, who was leaned back in the chair with her eyes closed. She looked exhausted, with circles under her eyes and swollen lids where she'd cried. "He's gonna be okay," Cole reassured her. "He's in good hands now."

She opened her eyes. "I know. Part of me is relieved and glad that we're here. The other part of me is now nervous for the diagnosis."

"Get some rest. You've been up all night, and it's nearly time for the sun to come up again."

"I will once Dr. Thorpe has come out to talk

to us." But she turned her weary head in his direction. "But thank you, Cole. You moved heaven and earth to get us here. I can never repay you. You're a good man."

Cole flushed under her praise, but the words that rang in his ears were the ones calling him a good man.

He was a successful man. A relatively smart man. A very rich man. But he wasn't sure he'd ever been called "good," and the compliment went straight to his heart.

He wanted to be a good man. And more accurately, he wanted to be a good man for her.

Wasn't life just full of surprises?

CHAPTER TEN

BROOKLYN NEVER DID fall asleep. It seemed hours until Dr. Thorpe came out and told them that Marvin had a foreign object in his stomach, and that he needed to do more tests. He further explained that exploratory surgery was most certainly necessary and as quickly as possible, to remove the blockage and ensure the fastest recovery. Brooklyn agreed right away, and Dr. Thorpe had disappeared to carry on.

Now she couldn't sleep. Not while she was waiting. She was exhausted, and sometimes she sat with her eyes closed, but that was only because her lids were so heavy. Her brain was too busy to close down, as well.

Cole didn't sleep, either. He sat next to her and held her hand. Dr. Thorpe had told them to feel free to use the coffee machine, and Cole got up and made her a cup of coffee and handed her the paper cup before making one for himself. Minutes ticked by, lots of them.

The sun came up, and at seven thirty one of the front office staff came in. "Oh," she said. "I didn't realize there was an emergency call. Do you need anything?"

"We're fine, thank you," Brooklyn said.

"Well, let me know. I came in to cancel today's appointments and to feed the animals we have kenneled in the back."

Finally, after what seemed an eternity, Dr. Thorpe returned with a smile on his face. "Good news. Turns out it was a bit of netting. We removed it and will watch him carefully for the next bit, run some fluids and make sure there are no complications. In a few days, he should be good as new."

Brooklyn let out a massive sigh of relief. This whole time she had been fighting against the thoughts about what she'd do without her beloved pet, but now that he was going to be okay the possibilities crowded her mind and she was both thankful and overwhelmed.

Cole stood and shook the vet's hand. "That's great news."

"Getting him here quickly helped. The sooner we can treat these issues, the better the prognosis. Marvin's in excellent health otherwise."

Brooklyn frowned, trying to think of what Marvin might have eaten and where. "Netting? I guess he might have picked it up on the beach. We do walk there every day. But I didn't notice him eating anything strange."

"It's hard to say. Dogs are like kids. The moment you have your back turned…" He grinned, and Brooklyn could see the tiredness behind his dark brown eyes.

"I can't thank you enough, Dr. Thorpe. Thank you for coming in and for having a generator." She smiled weakly.

"You're welcome. I'd like to keep Marvin here until tomorrow at least. Particularly where you're on the island, making sure he's good and stable is important. It's not like I live just around the corner."

"Of course. Whatever you think is best. Can I see him?"

"Certainly. He's still out, though."

Brooklyn went back and bit her lip when she saw Marvin resting, still unconscious from the anesthesia. His tongue hung out of his mouth, but his breaths were nice and even. She patted his head and gave him a kiss, and said a little prayer of thanks that he was going to be okay.

When she went out to the waiting room, Cole was chatting with the woman at the desk. "Hey," he said, smiling at her. "Jen says that power's out almost everywhere, but she heard that the lights are on at the Sandpiper Resort.

If they have a room, why don't we head there and get some sleep? That way you can be close to Marvin. If he can go home tomorrow, I'll have Dave fly us all home. If not, we can always fly back and bring a boat back to pick him up. But for today, you can get some sleep and not have to worry."

Right now she was so tired the thought of a comfortable bed nearly made her weep. "If they have a room, I'll say yes. I'm ready to drop."

"Same. Give me a few minutes to sort some arrangements."

He was looking after everything, and while she was thankful, it also felt a bit strange. She wasn't used to people taking charge and making sure her comforts were seen to. She wasn't quite sure how she felt about it really, or if her unsettled thoughts were all part of the emotion and fatigue of the past few hours. So she let it go, deciding they could talk about it later.

One cab ride later and he had them checked into the only room left at the Sandpiper. "We're lucky to have not lost power," the woman behind the desk said with a smile. "But that also means we're full up. You got our last room."

"Perfect." Cole sent her a winning smile and then held out his hand to Brooklyn. "Shall we?"

The only room left was of course the suite,

complete with a patio overlooking the ocean and a massive king-size bed with six pillows and a silk duvet that looked like a fluffy cloud. "Big enough for the both of us," Cole said, his voice utterly practical. "What do you want first? Sleep or food?"

Brooklyn yawned. "Sleep."

"Then in you go." He pulled down the covers and she crawled inside, fully clothed. The mattress felt absolutely heavenly, the pillow cradled her head perfectly. Her whole body melted into the fine linens.

"You're going to sleep too, right?" she asked, closing her eyes.

"You bet I am."

"Okay. Good." She was starting to drift off when she said, "Cole?"

"Yes, Brooklyn?"

"Thank you. So very much. I couldn't bear to lose him."

"I know. Sleep now."

She thought she felt his fingers brush the hair off her face. And then she remembered nothing.

When she woke, it was to the sensation of something warm pressed up against her back. She blinked against the brightness of the room—they hadn't bothered to shut the curtains—and remembered that she was in a gorgeous hotel suite with Cole. And that it was Cole who was spooning her right now, his breaths deep and even against her ear.

Brooklyn didn't want to move, it felt so good.

A few short weeks ago he'd come to the island with all intentions of getting her to sell her house. Now he was snuggled up next to her, after they'd weathered a hurricane together and he'd singlehandedly saved her best friend.

Because if they hadn't gotten Marvin prompt attention, the outcome might have been very different.

She'd had him pegged as an entitled, spoiled, rich jerk, but he hadn't borne out that initial impression. Indeed, he was caring and funny and generous.

And, boy, did he know how to kiss.

He snuffled a bit behind her and shifted, and she let out a sigh. His hand moved over her arm, and she hummed a little at the soft, soothing touch. When was the last time someone had casually grazed her arm like that? Or held her? She hadn't let anyone this close in years. Especially physically. It had only taken a few brief minutes on a spring afternoon to instill an aversion to having her space invaded. The attack had made it impossible for her to be intimate with anyone. But now she felt no panic. She hadn't on the beach the other night, either. All she felt with Cole was safe and protected.

Well, perhaps more than that.

"Did you get some rest?"

His voice sent ripples of pleasure down her spine. "I did, thank you."

"Good. You needed it."

She rolled over to face him, and was suddenly aware of the room they occupied. She'd been too tired and overwrought earlier, but now she realized that the suite they were in was stunning. It was probably nothing next to Cole's regular accommodations, but to her the huge space, luxurious bed linens and sweeping views were nothing short of amazing. She could never afford a night in a place like this on her own.

She definitely didn't want him thinking she expected it or…worse, that she was taking advantage. "Cole, I want to pay my share of the room." She didn't mention the helicopter ride or the cabs, though. They were both aware of the differences in their lifestyles. She wished she could afford to split the cost straight down the middle, but her finances would never withstand it. Instead, she'd feel forever in his debt. She didn't like that. Didn't like feeling indebted to anyone.

He studied her for a long moment, then nodded. "If you feel you must, but it's not necessary, okay? I would have done the same for any friend."

She believed him. And not just because it assuaged her guilt, but because Cole was turning out to be the kind of man who told the truth. "Any friend?" she asked. She seriously doubted Cole's friends ever needed this sort of help.

He smiled at her, his eyes still a little soft from sleep. "To show you I mean it, I'll share a funny story. I was traveling for work but found out that Jeremy was back in New York, licking his wounds because Tori had left him. I dropped everything, hopped on a plane and then Branson and I showed up at Jeremy's office and staged a romantic intervention."

She snorted a little. The picture of the two men offering relationship advice to Jeremy seemed utterly unreal. And yet… Jeremy and Tori were very happy. "I'm trying to imagine that."

"It really happened. He was miserable and taking it out on everyone around him. Anyway, I told you so you can see that I mean it, Brooklyn. When people are important to me, it's a pleasure to be able to help them." His eyes darkened. "Sometimes I wonder what I can possibly do with all my money. Helping friends is a good start."

Still, one thing stuck with her. "We're friends?"

A slow smile crept up his cheek. She was beneath the covers and he was on top, but it felt intimate just the same. "Aren't we?"

"I suppose we are," she conceded. "It's just unexpected."

"For me, too. But I'm not sorry."

She waited a few moments, trying to put her thoughts into words that wouldn't offend him. Finally, she met his gaze. "You're much nicer than I expected."

"Thank you?" He phrased it as a question. "Glad you think I'm nice. Not sure I'm as glad you didn't think so in the beginning."

She laughed softly. How lovely was it that they were still facing each other, talking? Was this what her grandmother had used to call "sweet nothings?"

"I had this idea of who you were. Especially after some of the things you said at first, about working hard and playing hard, and offering to buy me out without batting an eye at the price. You're in your mid-thirties, and not married. No girlfriend you've mentioned. I had this image in my head of a playboy, but that isn't being borne out by your behavior."

His smile widened. "Oh, I'm glad." His hand was still on her arm and his thumb made little circles. She wasn't even sure he knew he was doing it. "Here's the thing, Brooklyn. I did work hard and play hard for a lot of years. But things changed after my heart scare. I'd been trying so hard to be like my dad in some ways and very unlike him in others. I wanted to follow in his footsteps at Abbott, but I was determined to stay away from marriage, since he and my mother barely spoke. In the end, he died a young man because he was a workaholic. That is not a path I'd like to follow."

"Do you feel you've let him down somehow by slowing down, or adjusting your priorities?"

His eyes widened in acknowledgment. "Man, you hit the nail on the head. I do. Abbott Industries was everything to him. He was so damned good at it. I made a different choice, and on one level I know it was the right one. But I still haven't quite moved past the idea that I've failed or something."

"There's nothing wrong with searching for some balance in life. Or…getting off the hamster wheel."

"Intellectually I know that. I guess…" He halted, looked down and then lifted his gaze again. "I've always been looking for approval. My parents didn't have a good marriage. Certainly not overtly loving, and I'm an only child. It always seemed Dad's hopes were pinned on me. There was never any question of me not taking over the business. It was just a matter of when."

"And you're okay with that? Didn't you ever want to do something else?"

He smiled a little. "I went through a stage where I wanted to be a football quarterback. And then one where I thought I should be in a rock band. But seriously...no. I love the company. I want to see it succeed. And yet..."

His voice trailed away, and Brooklyn reached out to touch his cheek. "What is it?"

"Dad was a workaholic in an unworkable marriage. I don't want that for myself. So... I've never been much for relationships. I mean, that's just setting myself up for failure, isn't it? And I'm desperately trying to find the right balance so I can keep Abbott strong enough to withstand this economy, without putting myself in the hospital."

"Good thing you don't have high expectations of yourself, then," she quipped and smiled. "That's a lot of pressure on one person."

"I have a lot of responsibilities."

Brooklyn didn't quite get that, because she had deliberately set up her own life to be simple. Perhaps too simple, really. She loved the island, but was it enough to keep her through all her days?

When Cole had arrived on the island, she'd wanted nothing more than to keep everything exactly the same. But was that reasonable? Staying exactly the same meant she'd never be married, or have children of her own. She'd live alone in her grandparents' house and what, knit for the rest of her life?

"What is it?" Cole asked. "You suddenly looked very sad."

"Nothing, really. Just realizing how life carries us along with it no matter what we plan."

Before he could ask her what she meant, her phone buzzed. Grateful for the interruption, she rolled over and retrieved it from the table beside the bed. Dr. Thorpe had sent through a photo of Marvin, who was awake and apparently very groggy.

Power's on for real and Marvin's awake.

He'd punctuated it with a smiley face.

"Look," she said, rolling back and showing him the screen. "Marvin's loopy but conscious." She felt so much relief she was lightheaded with it. "Again, thank you so much."

"Turns out this has worked out okay for me,"

he said softly, brushing a piece of her hair behind her ear. "I'm here with you, aren't I?"

And yet his words about not wanting a relationship still echoed. Brooklyn struggled to define what was happening between them. They were neighbors. Friends. She wasn't exactly poor, but she had a very modest existence next to his lavish one. He had a high-powered career and she made a small living out of what had been a hobby. Their lives intersected in one small way—being on the island at the same time. But that was it.

So what did she want from this moment, right now, in a hotel room? It wasn't sex. Not that she didn't think it would be spectacular, because after what had happened on the beach she was sure there would be fireworks. But it would also make her incredibly vulnerable, and she wasn't ready for that. Not when there was no future in it.

"Cole…"

"Don't say it. I can see it on your face, and it's okay. Let's just get up, order some food and figure out what's next."

He wasn't going to push. She appreciated it and respected him for it. She was also a little disappointed in herself. Why was it so hard to reach out and take the opportunity before her?

Her throat tightened. The answer was simple, but certainly not easy to acknowledge. The truth was, one afternoon out of her lifetime had changed everything. It had made her seek guarantees, and in the absence of guarantees, she couldn't bring herself to take chances. And that was okay, wasn't it? Everyone made choices based on past experiences. After all, Cole had made several choices based on his upbringing and his father's death. He'd just said so.

Moreover, the only guarantee she wanted from him was that he'd leave her property alone, and he'd essentially done that already.

So she smiled as Cole rolled off the bed and reached for the in-room dining menu. In a matter of hours she'd be taking Marvin back home and life would get back to normal, wouldn't it? And despite her recent "is this all there is" thoughts, she was at least happy that she'd had the power to make those choices for herself.

Cole ordered up a feast of brunch foods: omelets, home fries, crisp bacon, a fruit platter with ripe berries, grapes and melon, pastries, and lots of coffee.

When their bellies were full, they ventured outside to the mile-long beach and listened to the pounding surf left over from the storm. The sun had come out, but there was a mess of driftwood and seaweed strewn behind on the normally pristine white sand. The crisp breeze was invigorating, and when they returned to the resort, they learned from the staff that power was slowly being restored across the province.

The island was sure to still be without, but she could manage with the generator—

The generator! In her haste last night, she'd forgotten to start it up at the house. Now it had been twenty-four hours and her fridge and freezer were sure to be thawed. Dammit! All her food would be wasted.

When she said as much to Cole, he frowned and fired off a text to Dan.

"It's too late," she lamented. "Dan can't do anything, Cole. It should have been done first thing this morning at the latest. I was planning on returning home this morning and starting it up if the power wasn't back on."

But Cole merely smiled and handed over his phone.

Thought of it and went to the house this morning. Damage is minimal and the generator's working fine. Will refuel it tonight.

She stared at the screen. "Dan did that?"

"Apparently. See? Nothing to worry about."

It had been so long since she'd relied on anyone, or even had someone look after her welfare, that she wasn't sure what to say.

"Have you checked your email or anything?"

She shook her head. "No. I've been trying to save battery." Indeed, her phone was now down to 32 percent. "And my data."

"I was going to check mine back in the room." He looked down at her and took her hand. The wind was cool in the aftermath of the storm, the tropical humidity gone from the air and leaving a distinctive fall feeling behind. "I'm sure they'll have charge cords at the desk. Unless you want to go home tonight. I can put Dave on standby."

She hadn't even thought of Dave. "Oh my gosh, is he still at the airstrip?"

Cole chuckled. "No. I sent him back to Halifax just after you went to sleep. Whenever we need him, he can be back here in a few hours. If you want to go home tonight..."

They could go back to the island. She could always return for Marvin with the boat tomorrow. It would be rough sailing, but the seas would be calmer than today. Or they could stay at the resort tonight and take Marvin home tomorrow if he was ready.

It would mean spending the night with Cole...

"I've got the room for the night anyway, Brooklyn, so it's entirely up to you."

There was only one bed. It was a giant one, but...

Cole sighed and looked out over the water. Brooklyn wasn't sure what to make of the dejected sound. Was he frustrated with her? With the situation?

"It's entirely up to you," she offered. "You've been so kind already. I will work around whatever it is you want."

He didn't look at her. "What I want is you. I told you that once before. So keep that in mind when you decide if you want to go home tonight or if you want to stay."

Then he turned his head to look at her. "I want you, Brooklyn. Even if it's for one night only."

That was it, then. He still wasn't looking for a relationship or anything more than a fling. The only thing left to decide was if she was willing to accept one night in his bed, or if she would protect her heart and her body and do the safe and sensible thing.

CHAPTER ELEVEN

COLE SAW THE struggle on Brooklyn's face and mentally prepared himself to call Dave and ask for a return flight to the island.

She liked him. He knew that for sure. But he also knew she was the kind of woman who played it safe. The walk on the dunes the other night had been an exception to the rule, but it had given him a taste of what she could be like when she dropped her guard and let her passion out to play.

He liked that woman a lot. He liked her anyway, but that night was branded on his memory with its sweetness and vulnerability and trust.

But when it was over, he'd sensed that it wasn't something to be repeated. And he might have promised her that nothing would happen tonight if they stayed. Nothing *would* happen if she didn't wish it. But he wasn't going to pretend that he didn't want it to. Because he did. He wanted to be with her, hear her say his name, feel her body against his. He wanted to be held in her arms, hear her throaty laughter in the dark. The choice was hers.

She met his gaze, her blue eyes troubled. "I don't know how to… I mean, I…" she stammered. "Cole, I don't know how to be casual, or…damn. I don't know how to say this without it sounding prudish or judgy or old-fashioned. It's not about that, really. It's more…"

She stopped again, and his heart softened. "Being vulnerable. Or…perhaps separating the physical from the emotional." Her cheeks reddened. "That's probably as good an explanation as any."

"And because we both avoid the word *love* like the plague."

She laughed a little, and he was glad. Facing this head-on was probably the right thing. Ignoring things unsaid would only lead to a mess.

"Well, that, too." She bit her lip for a moment before speaking again. "We have very different lives. They've intersected while you've been on the island, but let's not pretend that we actually exist in each other's spheres, both geographically and socially. What's between us…maybe it's real or maybe it's purely situational. But I… I'm not sure I can do sex in a situational way."

He nodded, disappointed but knowing he'd get over it. "I'm more than walking hormones," he replied. "I won't deny that I'm very attracted to you. But nothing will happen that you don't want to happen, if that's what you're worried about. You're very much in control, here, Brooklyn. Heck, there's a sofa. If you want, I'll sleep there. Or another room might free up for tonight." He put his hand along her cheek, the skin smooth and cool from the ocean breeze. "Whatever you want, that's what you'll have."

"What I want isn't fair." Her hair whipped around her cheek and she raised her hand to tuck it away. "I want to kiss you right now, right after saying that we can't be together. I'm a big mess of mixed signals, and I know it. But I think I'd like to stay, and we can take Marvin home tomorrow. If that's okay."

"Of course it's okay." His heart was pounding against his ribs, from wanting her, from her acknowledgment of wanting him, too. "And fair or not, I want to kiss you, too."

He put his other hand on her face so that she was cupped in his palms like a precious chalice. Then he leaned forward and kissed her. Her lips were cold but the inside of her mouth was soft and warm, and his body responded to the sweetness of the kiss.

Staying in the same room with her, in the same bed, would be torture. But one he was willing to undergo if it meant a few stolen kisses and the feel of her in his arms.

He ended the kiss and sat back on his heels, stunned by the sudden realization.

It wasn't just wanting her. It was about intimacy, and connection, and something far more substantial than a night in a hotel room.

It scared him half to death, and for a moment he considered calling the pilot and going back today anyway.

And then he looked at her shining eyes and left his phone in his pocket.

After their walk, they took a shower—separately. Neither had a change of clothes, but there were plush robes in the closet and they put those on instead. Cole tried to ignore the soft aloe scent of her damp hair, freshly washed with the hotel-supplied toiletries, but he wasn't having much luck. It seemed as if everything about her assaulted his senses. The fresh scent of her post-shower, her hair, darker when wet, and curling around her shoulders. If he touched her, it would be game over for him. The white robe, her skin, still pink from the hot water in the shower... If he touched her, would she make that little sound of pleasure like she had the night on the beach?

He busied himself with the menu again and they chose dinner items. He was pleased to see the inspired offerings on the dinner menu. Maple ginger salmon was paired with a sweet potato and bulgur dish as well as miso-roasted Brussels sprouts, and he ordered a bottle of Riesling to go with it. When dinner came, the wait staff set it up on the table in the seating area. Cole looked over at Brooklyn, who was watching the whole thing with wide eyes. He wondered if she'd ever had room service before today. If she had slipped into a hotel robe or enjoyed the finer things that she so obviously deserved.

He tipped the staff generously and then turned to Brooklyn. "Shall we?"

She giggled a little. "Oh, Cole! They saw us in our robes. Do you suppose they think that we…? Oh, my."

He chuckled. "So what if they did? I'm pretty sure it's not the first time. Come on, let's eat. This smells incredible. Tori was right. This inn is a hidden gem. What a gorgeous place."

She stepped forward then, and he lifted the dome off the plated meal. The colors, presentation, aroma…his stomach growled in response. Then he held her chair for her until she sat down. Just because they were in a hotel room didn't mean he'd lost his manners.

"Tori used to work here, right?"

Cole took his seat. "Yes, that's right. It's how she and Jeremy met."

Fork in hand, Brooklyn met his gaze. "I'd think your speed is more like…the Plaza. Or what's the other one in New York? The Waldorf Astoria."

She was so adorable. He wished he could take her there. Maybe he could. He had to go back to Manhattan soon; he couldn't avoid the Abbott offices forever. What if she went with him for a taste of the Big Apple?

"You've never been to New York, have you?"

She shook her head. "I've never been much of anywhere." She popped half of a sprout into her mouth and closed her eyes. "Oh, wow. I don't even really like Brussels sprouts and this is delicious. Not bitter at all."

He tried one, as well, and flavor exploded on his tongue. "You know," he said, after he'd swallowed the bite, "I'm really no different in New York than I am here. Maybe more relaxed, I suppose, but the same person. I don't go through a personality change."

She nodded. "I'm glad to hear it. Still, this isn't the life you're used to."

"Maybe it's better."

Where had that thought come from?

She laughed. "Do you really think so? It's a different lifestyle here. Slower, yes, but don't you miss, I don't know, theater and restaurants and…whatever it is you usually do?"

"You mean work in my office until nine p.m.? Hate to break it to you, Brooklyn, but last night, playing cards and having a few drinks? I don't remember when I last had that much fun."

He lifted his glass. "So why don't we toast? To simpler lives and happier times."

She raised her glass and touched the rim to his, her eyes glowing in the mellow light from the nearby lamp. They each took a sip.

"And to Marvin," she added.

He grinned. "Of course." They drank again. "And to making the best of a bad situation," he finished. "Because a private dinner for two is a heck of a nice way to spend the day after a hurricane."

"Cole…"

"Eat," he said softly. "Honestly, I don't care if we watch a movie and raid the snacks in the minibar. I'm just happy to be spending the evening with you, Brooklyn."

That much, at least, was 100 percent true.

Brooklyn savored each bite of the amazing dinner and every last drop of the Riesling.

Now she was warm and full and, if she were honest, seriously reconsidering her words of the afternoon.

Cole looked so approachable in the robe that all she wanted to do was untie the belt at his hips and see what happened. She wasn't brave enough, but it didn't stop her body from being hyperaware of his. He was across the room right now and she was already imagining what it would feel like to have his skin against hers.

She wasn't a virgin, but it had been a very long time, and truthfully she was starting to care for Cole—a lot. He would walk away one of these days and she knew the island would be lonely without him. If they were to indulge themselves—and it certainly would be nothing more than an indulgence—she wasn't sure she could untangle her emotions from the act, and that would leave her not just lonely but potentially desolate.

But oh, the temptation was very, very real.

The awareness only intensified as they found a movie on TV and got into the bed to watch it. It was a legal drama, and Brooklyn found herself caught up in the story line. At one point Cole paused it and got up to get refreshments. There was a small bottle of prosecco that Brooklyn thought sounded nice, so he did the honors and popped the cork for her, then fixed himself a drink from the small bottles and mix. There were snacks, too—nuts and chips and chocolate. He brought an assortment over and put it on the bed between them, shot her a boyish grin and plopped back into the bed. The movie continued and Brooklyn stole glances at him, contentedly munching potato chips and sipping on whatever he'd mixed with his soda.

The prosecco fizzed lightly on her tongue, slightly sweet but not overpowering. The air in the room changed, however, when the main characters of the movie escaped danger and found themselves alone, full of adrenaline, and gratitude for being alive.

Cole shifted slightly on the bed, but Brooklyn couldn't look over. She refilled her glass with the rest of the prosecco and tried to ignore her intense awareness of Cole at the moment, instead focusing on the screen. But that only made things worse. That Cole remained equally silent ratcheted the tension up another notch. Was he feeling it, too? That undeniable pull, made tighter by what was happening on screen?

She stole a glance at him and found him watching her. But he didn't move, didn't speak. He had said today on the beach that she was in control. At the time she'd thought it was control to say no, to keep things platonic. But now that word, *control*, took on a whole other meaning.

If she wanted something to happen, it could. And it could happen how she wanted it to. Everything was within her reach. All she had to do was reach out and grasp it.

She might not have another chance. She'd set her life up as she wanted. Why couldn't she have this one night to remember?

The scene switched, but Brooklyn reached for the remote and hit the mute button, sending the room into silence. Cole's neck bobbed as he swallowed, but he didn't move, didn't shift his gaze. Her stomach was a tangle of anxiety and anticipation, but she took a breath and lifted her chin.

Control. Power. Maybe it was finally time to reclaim hers.

She shifted and knelt on the bed, then reached for the tie on Cole's robe and tugged it gently. The knot fell away easily, and she reached down and opened the robe. Glory, he was beautiful, all lean muscle and definitely ready for her. Still he remained silent, as if speaking would break the tenuous spell.

Then she reached for the belt on her robe and undid it. Fear spiked... Long time, new man, lights on, and even a little body insecurity all played into her nervousness. But her need and longing overrode the sensation, and she let the robe gape open. Neither of them wore anything beneath the soft fabric, so they were not quite naked but were undressed all the same.

"Brooklyn," he finally whispered. "I don't... I can't..."

She loved that he was struggling to put words together. He was normally so self-assured, knowing exactly what to say. The feminine power of the moment seeped into her, emboldening her. She moved forward until her knees were next to his thighs. Then she slid her right leg over his so that she was straddling him, their bodies close together but not joined. Everything in her was crying out for completion, but she'd be damned if she'd hurry.

Control.

"Touch me," she said quietly, her voice roughened by desire. "Please, Cole. I'm dying for you to touch me."

"Show me where," he said, and she thrilled at taking the lead.

Brooklyn reached for his hand and guided it to her breast, loving the feel of his warm fingers against the sensitive skin. Her eyes closed for a moment as she absorbed the sensation, the tenderness of it, imprinting onto her memory the look of awe on his face as she'd opened her robe. She felt utterly beautiful and desirable, and free to take whatever she needed or wanted.

And what she wanted was what he wanted, wasn't it? She reached down and touched him, heard the harsh hiss of his breath as he inhaled. She opened her eyes only to find his closed, his head back against the pillow, strain tightening his face. All because she was touching him. His hips nudged against her and there was a fleeting feeling that this couldn't be real.

To prove she was wrong, she shifted and then settled, and they both stilled, struck by the magnitude of what she'd just done.

It was more than need. More than desire. It was…right. Like something clicked into place in that moment, key to lock. Her heart trembled as Cole's eyes opened and found hers. "Brook," he whispered, and tears stung the backs of her eyes.

She would not cry, even though this was the most beautiful moment she could ever remember.

Instead she started to move, dying to use this unexpected power to give him pleasure.

In the end the pleasure was mutual. Her robe slid off her shoulders and pooled at her hips. Skin grew slick and breaths quickened; he said her name and she called his in response. And yet they took their time and made it last, hovering on the edge of bliss as if they knew this was their one and only time. And when the final edges of their restraint frayed, any semblance of control was lost as they toppled into the unknown together.

CHAPTER TWELVE

THE ROOM WAS gray when Brooklyn woke the next morning. Last night they'd at least remembered to close the drapes to the room, and there was nothing but silence as her eyes adjusted to the dim light that entered through a sliver of window. Cole was asleep next to her, and neither of them was wearing a stitch of clothing. She'd slept naked with him…all night.

Now that day was dawning, reality poked its annoying head into the room. Today they would put on yesterday's clothes, and pick up Marvin, and fly back to the island and home.

She didn't want it to be over. Not yet. There was something so wildly wonderful about being in this bed with him, right now, away from both his world and hers, and in a world where it was just the two of them. She wanted to hang on to it a little longer, because that pesky reality kept wanting to have its say and she didn't want to listen. She'd have to, but not quite yet.

She shifted and the sheets brushed over her sensitive skin. Cole's lashes fluttered and she slipped her hand over his ribs, grazing the skin with her fingertips. "Mmm…" he murmured, eyes still closed. Her hand drifted lower and a smile teased the corner of his lips.

This time she let him have control, and she willingly surrendered to his desires. He didn't speak and neither did she; they let their bodies do the talking. There wasn't an inch of her now that he didn't know, and the thought was both wonderful and overwhelming.

She wasn't sure they could stay just neighbors after this. And wasn't sure where that left them, either. Not together, but with this *thing* between them, always making it more.

Cole kissed her forehead and slid out of the bed to turn on the shower, and Brooklyn stared at the ceiling. This couldn't happen again. Somehow they'd have to go back to being neighbors, wouldn't they? And only through part of the year. Somehow she had to find a way to put them back on even terms where he could carry on with his life and she with hers…

Then again, maybe it wouldn't be that hard for him. After all, he did admit that he'd played hard in years past, which translated to no serious relationships. There was no reason to think this would be anything different. Heck, even yesterday he'd said he avoided relationships because of his parents' marriage. She was making a big something out of nothing. Or, as Gram would say, there was no need to borrow trouble until trouble borrowed you.

She waited for him to finish showering, then took her turn while he called Dave and set up a pick-up time for around noon. Instead of room service, they checked out and grabbed coffee and pastries at the inn coffee shop. Then it was off to the clinic in a taxi.

The clinic was back in business, which meant the waiting room was full of clients and dogs on leashes and cats in carriers. Brooklyn was suddenly nervous about Marvin, and taking him home. He'd had surgery, so was it really okay for him to be going home so early?

Dr. Thorpe popped out from the back of the clinic and beckoned for them to follow him through. There they found Marvin, moving slowly but with a steadily wagging tail and a happy-dog smile on his face.

"Hello, my boy." She knelt down and he came over, nudging her shoulder with his wide head, begging for pats. She couldn't stop the grin from spreading over her face, and she leaned back and caught his head in her hands.

"Look, you crazy dog, don't go eating random stuff and scaring us again, huh?"

He licked her face.

Her cheeks flared as she realized she'd said "us" instead of "me," as if she and Cole were a couple.

Cole voiced the question that was on her mind. "Are you sure it's okay for him to go home?"

Dr. Thorpe nodded as Brooklyn got to her feet. "We could keep him another night, but he's doing well. I've got some medication for you to take with you, and a staff member will go over it with you, but he's young and healthy. I don't see any reason to expect complications. He needs to take it easy, though. For at least a week or two. No big runs on the beach. His stomach is bound to be touchy, too, so a bland diet is a good idea until he's healed. Mostly he just needs love and rest at this point."

"Love won't be an issue," Brooklyn assured him. She was fairly swamped with gratitude. "And I'll keep him on leash until he's good to go."

"If anything happens, we can be here fairly quickly." Cole spoke up, his voice quiet but with authority. "I've got to head back to New York in a few days, but my caretaker will be at the house and I'll keep the pilot on standby."

Dr. Thorpe grinned. "First patient I've ever had with his own air ambulance."

Brooklyn was still reeling from what Cole had just said. Not about the helicopter; at this point she was no longer surprised at his generosity. But he hadn't mentioned a word about going to New York. Of course, she'd known it would happen eventually, but he must have known before…

She swallowed tightly. Before last night.

She didn't feel duped, exactly, but there was no denying that if she'd known, she might have thought twice about sleeping with him. And there was definitely a niggle of doubt where he was concerned. Had he kept that little detail to himself because he suspected she would shut him down?

"Thank you so much, Dr. Thorpe."

"No problem at all. Call if you have any concerns or questions, okay?"

She walked Marvin out to the waiting room and then got all the paperwork and instructions from the assistant at the desk. She also pulled out her credit card to pay the bill, but the invoice showed a balance of zero.

She looked up at Cole. "You paid my vet bill?"

"If you're mad about it, we can talk. You can always pay me back."

"I will." She lifted her chin. He'd been a wonderful help, but he'd taken over a lot, too. She still had some pride. And that pride was stinging over his lack of disclosure. "Marvin's my dog, and I'm responsible for him."

"Okay, then." He said it easily, maybe too easily. They left the clinic and got into the waiting cab. Brooklyn's emotions were all over the place. She needed to pay her own way, but the vet bill and her half of the hotel bill would definitely take a chunk out of her small savings. But she didn't want his help, either. Didn't want their friendship to be predicated on whether or not he paid for things. Or…feeling constantly indebted.

This was the problem, wasn't it? Before, they were just friendly, getting along as neighbors. Now it was different. In the beginning, she'd let him pay for the dock because legally she could have made it difficult for him to make changes. That was business. This was…well, if not pleasure, it was personal. It changed the dynamic between them and she didn't like it.

Maybe it was better that he went back to New York now, so they could stop pretending they had something real.

"You're awfully quiet," he said, looking past Marvin's head to catch her gaze.

"Just thinking. There's a lot to do when I get

back. I don't even know if I have power back.
This morning the news was that some parts of
the province might not get it back for three or
four more days."

"As long as you have lots of gas for your
generator, you'll be fine."

"I know."

She hadn't even been thinking about the
practicalities, but she wasn't going to tell him
that.

All too soon the drive to the airstrip was
over and their helicopter was waiting. Cole
lifted Marvin out of the car but the dog walked
to the chopper under his own steam. Then Cole
lifted him up again, careful of his incision.

When everyone was secured, Dave readied
for takeoff and Brooklyn let out a long breath.
Once she was home she'd find the inflatable
collar that she'd used the last time Marvin had
had stitches, to keep him from licking. It was
a little friendlier than a huge cone. Then she'd
cook up some rice and chicken for him to eat
until his stomach healed. She nuzzled his face
with her nose. "I'm so glad you're okay, buddy.
You scared me."

A happy lick was her reward.

Once they were airborne, Brooklyn got a
good look at the devastation from the hurricane. Structures were mostly fine, but it was

easy to see downed trees, and as they got to the coast, the mess left behind from the storm surge. She remembered that she had a huge tree in her lane that would need to be dealt with. In years past her dad would have made the trip with his chainsaw and they all would have hung out together. Maybe she'd give him a call and see if they wanted to make the trip from Halifax.

She let out a hefty sigh.

"What is it?" Cole reached over and touched her shoulder.

"Just a lot to do, that's all. But thank you so much, Cole. If not for you, Marvin could have died before I could get him to the mainland. I appreciate this more than you know."

"Maybe you can show your appreciation later." He smiled at her, his eyes twinkling. They had their headsets on, and she saw Dave smile a little in the cockpit.

She wasn't going to answer. If they were to have a conversation, it wouldn't be in the air with a pilot listening in.

Dan and Raelynn were waiting when they landed, and Brooklyn was surprised at the feeling of pleasure she got, to see them waving at her. Dan came forward and helped Cole get Marvin out of the helicopter, and Raelynn practically showered the pup with kisses. "Oh, here's a good boy." She kissed his head and ruffled his ears. "I'm so glad he's okay, Brooklyn."

"Me, too. I'm sure he'll be up to no good before I know it."

Dan came forward and gave her a small hug. "Your generator's still working fine. Latest update is that we'll have power back tomorrow."

"Thank you, Dan. I appreciate that more than you know."

"It was no problem at all."

There was an awkward silence while they all stood there, as if wondering what to do next. Brooklyn finally jolted into action when Marvin pulled on the leash. "I'd better get this guy home. Plus, I'm dying for a change of clothes."

Cole thankfully took the bait. "Yes, me too. We left in kind of a hurry. I'll check in later, though, okay?"

"Sure," she responded, unsure of what exactly that meant or what she wanted it to mean. It was like last night was a whole world away, divorced from reality.

Cole changed into jeans and a soft sweater, then sat down to a delicious meal prepared by Raelynn. Their breakfast had been small and on the run, so he appreciated the homemade soup and substantial sandwich she placed on the table. Their internet was still down, so he was using his phone and eating up his data to work. Arrangements were being made for next week and his return to Manhattan. The first retreat at the house had gone well; one of his business acquaintances was planning a week here with his senior staff later in November. Granted, it wasn't the best time of year as far as weather and scenery, but Dan and Raelynn would make sure everyone was warm and cozy, and there was a facilitator coming with the group to guide their activities.

It was exactly what he'd bought this place for. And it would be much busier next summer.

He imagined Brooklyn here over the winter and wondered how she managed it. A good nor'easter would blow nearly as hard as the hurricane that had passed through, only colder and with snow, not rain. How did she manage being on the island alone for that?

What if…

He shook his head and spooned up more soup. No, it was ridiculous, wasn't it? She wouldn't leave the island. Unless… He thought back to last night and this morning, and the way she'd been in his arms. How she'd laughed playing cards, and the way she'd held his hand while they were waiting for news of Marvin. He cared about her so much. He might even… love her. It was a foreign idea in his brain; he'd never let himself even consider the word before. But Brooklyn was different, and the way he felt about her was different, too.

What if she came to New York for a while? It was still East Coast weather in the winter, but without the isolation. The more he thought about it, the more the idea had merit. She said she hadn't traveled, hadn't she? They could stay in his penthouse. Maybe do Thanksgiving at the family home in Connecticut. If it went well, she could go back in January or something, stay for a while. They could...

He sat back in his chair. What he was considering was having a relationship. And for the first time in his life, he wasn't afraid of the word.

How had this even happened?

Maybe because, for the first time, he'd been with a woman who he knew wasn't after his money. She'd turned it down, for Pete's sake! And had insisted on paying him back for the hotel and vet bills. She had so much pride. With Brooklyn, he got the feeling that his status worked against him, rather than for him... but she liked him anyway. She'd shared things with him, about her painful past. Was it possible she could love him, too?

"Are you all right, Cole?" Raelynn's voice interrupted his thoughts and he picked up his spoon again.

"Oh, yes, thank you. This is delicious."

"Brooklyn gave it to me last week. It's her grandmother's corn chowder recipe. I think her grandmother was a good cook from the sounds of it. I was thinking of asking her for more regional recipes for when I'm cooking for guests here."

"That's a great idea." Cole smiled up at her. "Thank you, Raelynn, for everything."

Raelynn's smile slipped, and she sat down in the chair next to him. "Cole, there's something I want to talk to you about, just to think about, of course."

Her face was tight with anxiety, her eyes worried. Cole frowned and pushed his near-empty bowl away. "What is it? Did something happen while we were gone?"

"No, not at all. We managed fine." She sent him a weak smile. "It's just…well, Dan would be upset if he knew I was talking to you, but I think it's only fair to be open and honest. The truth is…we've been talking about trying for a baby. You hired us here together, and I can still do the job after a short maternity leave, but it…might be on the radar in the near future."

That was all? He smiled at her. "Of course you two want a family. Are you pregnant already? Should I not have asked that?" He was unsure of the protocol of these things, but Rae-lynn's face relaxed at his reaction.

"No, not yet. I certainly wouldn't have in-dulged on the night of the storm if I had been. It's just that we both really like it here. And living above the garage is fine for the two of us—"

"But not for a baby."

"We could manage, but it's not optimal, no."

"Of course it's not." He had known that when they'd first arrived weeks ago, but there hadn't been a huge rush to make adjustments. There was probably room in the house, but he could also understand the couple wanting to have their own space for their family.

As far as the island went, Brooklyn's house was still the perfect solution. Except she wouldn't sell it…and she'd thanked him for letting the idea go. Which meant that idea was firmly off the table.

Unless it wasn't…

"Leave it with me," he said to Raelynn. "I'm sure we can come up with something. You're coming to New York for Thanksgiv-ing, though, aren't you? I'm sure your families would like to see you."

She nodded. "That's the plan, for now, any-way. Unless you need us here."

He already knew there were no events

planned for that weekend, and he would still be in New York. There was no reason for Dan and Raelynn to stay.

Which put Brooklyn here on the island alone—unless he could convince her to come along.

"I'll be back at dinner time," he announced, getting up from the table. "I'm going down to Brooklyn's to see how Marvin is settling in."

It wasn't subtle at all, and by the look on Raelynn's face, she wasn't buying it, either. He didn't really care. They needed to talk after this morning.

CHAPTER THIRTEEN

BROOKLYN EXPECTED COLE to show up, and he did, right around three o'clock. She'd settled Marvin and put his inflatable collar on. He looked ridiculous, but it kept him from being able to reach his incision and that was all that mattered.

The dog was pouting on his doggy bed and she'd changed into jeans and a warm sweater. She'd put on a pot of coffee. When she saw Cole walking down the lane, she reached into the cupboard and took out her special bottle of Irish cream. The conversation ahead might require a little fortification.

Marvin popped his head up when Cole knocked, but that was it. She answered the door and when they went back into the kitchen, Marvin's tail was thumping against the fabric of the bed. There now. He might not be himself, but he was happy to see Cole.

As she was. And that wasn't a good thing, she was thinking.

"Hey, buddy," Cole crooned, squatting before the bed. "How're you feeling, huh?"

Thump-thump.

"He's pouting about the collar," she offered and started pouring coffee.

Cole took the cup she offered. "I see you've got the necessities running off the generator."

"Fridge, freezer, water pump. And one power bar in the kitchen, for the microwave, coffee maker, and a lamp."

She held up the bottle of liqueur. "Care for some?"

"I wouldn't say no."

She put a splash in each mug. Irish cream coffee was a special treat she didn't indulge in often, but considering the craziness of the last few days, it seemed appropriate. "This reminds me of my granddad," she said, putting the cap back on the bottle. "He liked a drop in his coffee. We used to come over to the island on the weekends in the fall sometimes. He'd make his 'special' coffee, and we'd sit out on the front porch and smell the fall air."

"That sounds lovely." He looked into her eyes. "Would you like to sit out there now?"

She did, rather. She was feeling nostalgic this afternoon. Perhaps it was getting swept away for a few days, both in the emergency and the opulence of Cole's way of life. The storm had barely caused a blip at the mansion, and he'd merely had to snap his fingers to have a helicopter on its way, the last hotel room in town, room service. Maybe money couldn't buy happiness, but it could sure buy convenience.

It all seemed rather surreal now.

Marvin had settled into a snooze on the bed, so they went to the front verandah and sank into the cushions on the wicker chairs there. The wood creaked beneath their weight, and Brooklyn let out a sigh before she took a first sip of coffee and let memories wash over her. This had always been her happy place.

"Brooklyn, I came to talk about us."

She hadn't expected him to be so blunt. "Us?"

"Yes. Things have changed, wouldn't you agree?" When she didn't answer, he pressed on. "We spent the night together. That's not nothing. And it would be really great if you could look at me."

She did, the moment he said it. She lifted her gaze to his and felt that awful and wonderful turning in her stomach. He was in jeans and a sweater but it didn't matter. There was something in the way he carried himself, the way he spoke, that put him in another league. She was hard-pressed to pinpoint it, but she figured it fell into the category of "I know it when I see it." He had this presence about him that was confident but not arrogant, expensive but not ostentatious, and so very, very capable.

She could hold her own, but looking at him now, after what they'd shared, she found him a bit intimidating. Because any "us" would be horribly misbalanced, wouldn't it?

"It was one night, Cole. I'm not harboring any big expectations."

Was that disappointment on his face? She couldn't quite tell, but she could see by the tension around his eyes that her answer wasn't the one he'd been anticipating.

"I see." He took a sip of his coffee and then turned back to her again. "No, actually, I don't see. You don't strike me as the type to indulge in one-night flings, Brooklyn. I appreciate maybe you think you're letting me off the hook, but…" He cleared his throat. "But what if I don't want to be off the hook?"

Her breath caught. What was he saying? That he wanted them to be a thing? Have a relationship? That was ludicrous. They'd already decided things couldn't go further, that day he'd kissed her in the back porch.

And yet they had. They'd made love, twice. They'd passed "further" the moment she'd untied her robe and decided to follow her heart.

And that was it, wasn't it? Her heart was involved now. She truly, truly cared for him. And that was exactly why she had to walk away now. She would never fit into his life, and she didn't really want to. It would mean leaving this behind. The life she'd built for herself, by herself. She was a woman with a high school diploma from a tiny town, making a simple living. She had no business consorting with a billionaire, for Pete's sake.

"What do you want from me, Cole?"

He reached over and took her hand. "I want you to come to New York with me. I have to leave in the next few days and I know Marvin can't travel so soon, but I'd like for you to come stay with me when he's better. I don't want to say goodbye, Brooklyn. Not after last night. Not after everything. You make me laugh. I want to be near you all the time. And last night...that was so amazing." He put his cup down and turned his chair so he was facing her, and then clasped her other hand, too. "Please say yes. I care about you too much to say goodbye."

"You want a relationship with me." Her voice was tight and she couldn't quite sort out why. Any woman would be jumping for joy right about now. Why wasn't she?

"I want us to have a chance to explore

what's happening between us. And realistically, I can't stay on the island forever. I still have responsibilities. But you could come to my world, couldn't you?" His face was alight with enthusiasm. "Have you ever been to New York? I can take you so many places. The theater. Restaurants. Museums. Walking through Central Park with Marvin. Whatever you want to do."

Brooklyn frowned. Sure, it would be easy to get swept away, wouldn't it? It was a Cinderella dream come true, with the prince sitting here saying all the right things. But in fairy tales the princess was always ready to live in the castle. Brooklyn was sure she'd be a square peg in a round hole.

"I have work here, Cole. It is one of my busiest times, leading up to the holidays. I can't just jet off on a moment's notice." She met his gaze. "That's not how the real world works."

He frowned and sat back a little, perhaps a bit surprised at her sharpish tone. "So you can't dye your stuff in my penthouse," he reasoned. "But you could do everything else. Your business is online, right?"

"That's not the point."

"What is the point?"

She pulled her hands away. "The point is you expected me to jump up and say yes, I'd do what you wanted on a total whim, and when I didn't you're pouting."

"I do not pout."

She knew he wasn't pouting; he was genuinely confused and perhaps he had a right to be, considering what had happened last night. But she was already in it and it was too late to turn back now. "Yes, you are. You're used to getting what you want, and you think that my life is so insignificant that I can just pick up and leave because you've crooked your finger."

His mouth fell open. "When have I ever given you that impression?"

He hadn't, but panic was tightening her chest. The moment he'd stepped on the island, he'd threatened her very safe existence. She cared for him, she did. But it was a long way from there to relationship. Because who would be making all the sacrifices? She would.

"It's how you live, Cole. You pick up the phone and have a helicopter ready to take you where you want to go. You have a home in New York but it was nothing for you to drop more money than I'll ever make in a lifetime on this island, so you can have some sort of high-class retreat." She lifted her chin. "You are so used to getting what you want that you expected me to sell my home for the right price." A sudden thought took hold. "Maybe what you like in me is the challenge, because I'm probably the first person to say no to you in a very long time, huh? But what happens when that challenge is gone? Will you be bored of me then? And what's to become of me at that point?"

Cole looked stricken, and she had to turn away. She'd been harsh just now, even if her words had come from a place of real fear. She hadn't expected this invitation. Hadn't expected him to want...more.

Her friends would tell her she was crazy to not take a chance. They still believed in the fairy tale. But there was no security in those sorts of crazy dreams. If nothing else, Brooklyn considered herself a realist.

"I didn't realize you thought so little of me," he said quietly, his elbows resting on his knees. "And I thought you knew me better. I shared stuff about myself that I don't generally share with people, and I thought you understood. So if you think me asking you is because you're a challenge, you don't know me at all."

Her heart hurt, hearing the disappointment in his voice. "I would never fit into your life," she added, less angry now and more sad and practical. "We're from two different worlds, Cole. I'd be unhappy, I just know it. This is where I belong."

"I never said I wanted you to leave the island. Just to give us a chance. Brooklyn, I've never felt this way about anyone. You make me laugh, and you're the most genuine person I've ever met. I don't love you because you're a challenge. It's because you challenge me, and I need that. When I'm not with you I think about being with you. I made a commitment to balance my life better, and I think you were meant to be a part of that. Please, give this a chance."

The cramp in her chest went cold when he used the word *love*. Was that even possible? They'd known each other a matter of weeks. Did he even realize what he'd said? This was all spiraling too fast. "Cole, that's a big thing to say after we've spent one night together."

Hurt flashed across his face. "You surprise me. Yesterday we were walking the beach together. We shared something amazing. I can only guess that you're running scared right now, and that's okay. Believe me, I'm scared, too. I think the thing is, Brooklyn, I trust you. I believe that you're not interested in me because of my money. In fact, I think that point is working against me right now."

She couldn't deny it.

"I won't fit in there," she said firmly. "And you'd come to resent me. I shouldn't have let this go so far." She twisted her fingers together, knowing what she had to say and hating it just the same. "I shouldn't have slept with you, knowing we didn't have any sort of a future. Do you know, I wondered if you hadn't told me you were leaving because you thought if you did, last night, I would say no?"

"Exactly the opposite," he said roughly. "I didn't tell you because I was still sorting through my feelings, deciding what I wanted to do. Then I imagined you coming to visit me, see me in my world, and I thought…" He ran his hand through his hair. "Well. It doesn't matter what I thought. You don't want to have anything to do with my world. You only want island Cole, who stays in your safe and secure world, and doesn't make you take any risks, right?"

She sat back. "Hey."

"No, not hey. You basically just said that I used a lie of omission to get you into bed, and I resent that. A lot. We were friends, Brooklyn. At least I thought we were. We shared things with each other, things that we don't talk about often. Maybe you regret what happened last night, but I don't. My motives where you were concerned were pure. Can you say the same?"

Brooklyn bristled at that and pushed out of her chair, going to the verandah railing and clenching it in her fingers. "They weren't impure, if that's what you're getting at. I wasn't angling for something."

"Weren't you? What happened? Did you decide to go for it because it was low-risk? Because I was always going to be leaving? Or did you think I didn't care? Do you think I flew you and Marvin to the mainland so I could impress you with my money? I sincerely hope not. It was my way of helping a friend in need. Maybe I was wrong. I believed you thought better of me."

Tears threatened now. He was hurt and angry and she had never wanted any of those things. Except, she realized, the low-risk part. And that she'd never considered that he might be hurt by it. She hadn't considered his feelings, because she'd got so caught up in what he was and not who he was.

"You're right. Not about everything, but some things. And it shows we aren't right for each other. I'm sorry, Cole. That's all I can say. I'm sorry."

He sat for a moment in the silence that followed, then let out a long, slow sigh. Finally, he stood and faced her, his hands shoved into his jeans pockets.

"You disappoint me, Brooklyn. I'm surprised and disappointed."

God, of all the things to say. Those words

gutted her. She'd spent years trying to get over the feeling that she'd let people down. She'd dropped out of her degree. She'd stayed away from relationships. She'd hidden herself away on the island because it was her happy place but moreover, her safe place. And while there was nothing wrong with searching out safety and peace, she'd always felt as if by doing so she was somehow disappointing those who meant the most to her.

Cole stepped forward, close enough that she had to look up to meet his gaze, and her insides trembled as he fixed his eyes on hers.

"You are so much more than you think, but you hide away so no one sees it. It feels like building your life here is a solution, but it's really just a way of avoiding dealing with what happened to you. And I can say that because of some of the things I did when my dad died, and again during my own health scare." His voice gentled and he lifted one hand to touch her cheek. "It's the difference between avoiding life and embracing it. I decided to stop running a few days ago when I accepted my feelings for you. But I can't force you to make that same decision. You have to do it on your own time. Maybe you never will."

He dropped his hand and backed away. "I'll be going in a couple of days. Dan and Raelynn will be here until after the holiday. If you need anything, don't hesitate to ask them. Goodbye, Brooklyn."

She couldn't answer, not even to say goodbye. She was too dumbstruck, too floored by what he'd said. Every instinct within her wanted to shout out that he was wrong. That moving here was embracing life, the kind of life she wanted.

But deep down she knew that was a lie. He'd seen it and called her out on it.

Fine. Maybe hiding away here on the island wasn't the right thing, but that didn't mean jetting off to New York City was the answer, either.

Brooklyn watched him go until he was out of sight at the end of the lane, and then she went back inside. Marvin was still sleeping on his bed, and she looked around her little house. She loved it. She did feel safe here. But even with Marvin for company, it was lonely. Especially now, with Cole gone for good.

Tears stung her eyes but she rubbed them away. She wasn't going to cry over Cole Abbott and his hurtful words. And she definitely wasn't going to cry over the decisions she'd made.

She was a strong woman, despite what Cole said. And that meant she'd get over him, too.

* * *

Cole strode into the executive offices of Abbott Industries and smiled as he greeted the receptionist at the front desk. "Good morning, Jennifer," he said brightly, and she waved as the phone rang and she hit a button on her headset.

It was good to be back. At least in most ways it was. The break on the island had been wonderful—for the most part—and he'd recharged. Now, though, it was time to get back and get to work. He'd handled most things remotely during his absence, but there was a different energy in the office. One he'd missed, he realized.

But he wasn't going to lie to himself and say he had no regrets. And if they weren't exactly regrets, he had feelings about what had happened with Brooklyn that weighed on his mind. Because he'd meant every single thing he'd said to her that day on her porch. Including the fact that he loved her.

This was his third day in the office and he had meetings scheduled for half of his time. One meeting was with the executives who'd gone on the retreat, to follow up on both their personal and professional thoughts since coming back to the "real world." He was looking forward to that a lot.

But first, there was a personal meeting he had to get out of the way.

He greeted his executive assistant and then took a deep breath before turning the handle on the door to his expansive office with a splendid view of the Hudson.

His mother was sitting behind his desk.

"Hello, Cole," she said, her voice warm and yet very…polite. In her late fifties, she still looked young and vibrant, with artfully colored hair and perfect makeup. Allison Abbott was a woman who took care of herself, always.

At least, publicly. As Cole knew, her private life had always been quite a hot mess.

"Mother," he said, putting down his briefcase. "Thank you for coming."

"I assumed that was what one does when one is summoned."

That stung a little. Not because it wasn't true, but because that was the nature of their relationship. "I've been slammed since returning. I thought the office was the easiest way." He didn't mention that she never came here anymore since his father's death.

He went to the door again to ask for coffee to be brought in. Then he lifted an eyebrow and said, "Maybe we can sit over here. Instead of you being behind my desk."

She laughed then, a sound Cole was unused

to hearing. "Oh, Cole, I wondered if that would irritate you. You can be so stern."

Him? Stern? He hadn't considered it that way, but he supposed he came by the trait honestly. Still, he hoped he wasn't that way in all his personal relationships. Jeremy and Bran had never said such a thing. If anything, he'd prided himself a little too much on his social charm. Even if it did feel forced a lot of the time. It was one of the things he liked about Brooklyn, actually. He'd never had to put on a show. He'd been genuine, like he was with Bran and Jeremy, and Jess and Tori.

"You're very like your father in a lot of ways," she continued, and moved to sit on the small sofa in the rather huge office.

Cole's assistant brought in coffee and once they had fixed their cups, his mother looked up and asked, "Why did you call me here, Cole?"

He hesitated, lifting the cup to his lips and taking a revivifying sip while he considered his words.

"I want to talk about you and Dad."

She frowned. "What about us? Good heavens."

"I've never understood your relationship." His heartbeat quickened with nerves; this was a heck of a thing to talk about with one's mother.

"I never saw any affection between you. You never did things together. And I felt…"

He halted, pursed his lips.

"You felt what?"

He met her gaze. "In the way."

Her eyes softened with what looked to Cole like regret, and her lips turned down a little. "I'm sorry about that. Your father's and my relationship was…complicated." She put down her cup and rested her hands in her lap. "Why are you asking this now? Have you… met someone?"

"What does that have to do with anything?"

She gave a delicate scoff. "Oh, Cole, we both know that falling in love with someone makes us question everything."

There was something in her voice that gave him pause. She fiddled with her fingers once more and he noticed that they were ringless. She'd stopped wearing her wedding rings. While a tiny part of him wanted to be outraged on his father's behalf, he knew he couldn't be. They'd had a cold marriage. Why shouldn't she take off the rings?

Why hadn't they divorced? Lord knew enough of his friends had had divorced parents.

"That's an interesting comment, considering it never really seemed like you—" He paused, reconsidered his phrasing. "Like you and dad were in love."

Her gaze slid away for a moment. "We weren't. But it doesn't mean I don't know what love is, Cole. Don't be naive."

Of course. He was looking at all this through tunnel vision. He'd always considered his parents as, well, parents. Not exactly...people. Which was rather selfish of him, really. Brooklyn would tell him to keep an open mind, wouldn't she? That people hid all sorts of pain behind personal façades.

"I'm sorry, Mother. That was uncalled for."

"Not necessarily. I know we failed you. I wasn't happy, Cole, and it affected every part of my life. Including how I parented you. I was awful at it." She met his gaze again. "I was not a good mother. I don't think I really knew how desperately unhappy I was until I—" her cheeks pinkened "—well, until I was free to be happy."

"And now you are?"

She nodded. "Yes. Oh, Cole, if you hadn't called me to your office, I was going to come visit anyway. I have news for you."

She wore an expression he'd never seen before. It was warm and peaceful and happy, and took a good ten years off her face. "What is it?"

"I want to tell you I'm getting remarried," she said with an unexpected softness to her voice. "And I wanted you to know before anyone else."

He sat back. Of all the announcements, this was the last thing he expected. "Remarried? To whom?" His brain jumped back over the past few months. The rings were missing from her fingers. Had she been seeing anyone special? How had he missed it? Then again, he'd been on his own private island, hidden away from the world.

"It's Edward."

"Edward…?"

"Mowbry."

"Your lawyer?" Cole let out a huge breath. "Good God, when did this happen?"

She looked him in the eye and said, "Thirty years ago."

Cole put down his coffee before he could spill it. "Wait. I would have been—"

"Five." She held his gaze, never wavering. "So yes. It means I had an affair. Though I hate calling it an affair. It sounds so tawdry. I fell in love."

"Did Dad know?"

"Oh, he knew." Now that she'd made her announcement, she'd relaxed. She took a calm sip of her coffee. "Truthfully, Cole, we probably should never have married. His family had money, my family had money, we were in the right social sphere. And we liked each other well enough, but that's not enough to build a marriage on. We learned that very quickly."

"I don't know what to say." Cole was still trying to process everything. He'd idolized his dad, even though he'd often felt as if nothing he did was good enough. But they'd had their share of happy times. And Cole had soaked up every small bit of praise from his father like he was a man dying of thirst and his father's praise was lifesaving water. To learn she'd had an affair...

"I wasn't a good mother, and I can't change that," she said softly. "I was unhappy, and your father was always talking about you being the future of the company and it was like you were all that mattered and I was...nothing. When he found out about Edward, it was awful. He didn't speak to me for weeks."

"Why didn't you divorce him? If you were that unhappy?"

"Edward broke it off. And I didn't know how to do it on my own. Your dad would have put me through a horrible court case if I wanted any alimony. And he would never have allowed me to take you with me. So I stayed."

Cole sat there, his coffee cooling, his head

full of everything she was telling him, trying to sort through it all. Maybe she'd stayed, but she hadn't been a very good mother. Certainly not nurturing.

"Would you have wanted to take me?"

Tears filled her eyes. "Oh, yes. And maybe… I don't know. Maybe I would have been a better parent. Any time I suggested anything, your father told me I was wrong and that he knew what you needed. I suppose you'd say I should have kept trying…but the criticism and coldness got into my head. I told myself he was right. I didn't know how to parent you. Then he insisted you go away to school…"

Cole shook his head. "Don't regret that decision. Merrick was the most wonderful time of my life."

"I do regret it. You should have had a home to come to, rather than a boarding school being your home."

Silence fell as that truth settled.

"And now that you're free, you and Edward…"

"Yes. Me and Edward." She cleared her throat. "Cole, you had all sorts of material things and advantages, but you didn't have love and affection. I need to own that, and tell you I'm sorry I failed you. I was so desperately unhappy that I simply didn't have love to give.

And I was afraid if I ever let go of the tight control I had over my life, I'd fall apart and never be able to be put back together again."

Cole looked up abruptly and stared into his mother's face. He wondered if he should feel angry in this moment; after all, she was right. He had felt unloved through most of his childhood. And yet he was seeing his mother as another human being, with her own problems and stressors. And he knew that feeling of falling apart. How could he possibly sit in judgment of her and keep a clean conscience?

"It's okay," he said quietly. "Listen, I know what it's like to fall apart. And the good news is you can put yourself back together again. But I understand the fear. I really do."

"You should hate me. Or at least…not care. I came here expecting that."

It made him sad, that his mother would think such a thing. What a mess of a relationship they had.

"Mom, after Dad died, and I had taken over the corporation, I did fall apart. I didn't really say anything, and I made it seem as if I'd taken a much-needed vacation. Truthfully, I thought I had a heart attack and that scared the hell out of me. And then I went into a depression. Dad had worked himself to death, and I didn't want that for myself. It took that big scare for me to decide to not try to be a mirror image of my dad. It's why I bought the property in Nova Scotia. You'd like it there, I think. Gorgeous house, lovely beach…"

Wonderful neighbor. Best dog in the world. And the place where he'd left his heart behind.

"Anyway, my point is, there are worse things than falling apart." He smiled a little. "And I'm glad you told me. Wish you'd told me sooner."

"Your father wasn't a bad man, Cole. He just wasn't the man for me. And my unhappiness made me a poor excuse for a parent. That's not on your father, either. That's on me, and I'm sorry."

He hadn't expected the apology or the endorsement of his father. He'd guessed long ago that their marriage was one of appearances only. It was different hearing it articulated.

"So you really love Edward, huh?"

If he'd had any doubts, they evaporated when she smiled. Her eyes lit up and the lines of strain on her face melted away. "Oh, I do. He did get married, you know. And divorced. We crossed paths at an event months ago and it just…clicked. Like it had from the beginning."

Cole thought back to that first morning when he'd seen Brooklyn, expecting some middle-aged woman with a set of knitting needles in her hands, and instead being greeted by a woman with gorgeous waves of hair and shining eyes the color of an October sky. Yes, he could understand that "click" all too well.

He let out a breath. "But don't you worry that it'll… I don't know, be like before? That maybe you're…" His voice trailed away. "I'm sorry. I think I'm projecting onto you."

"Have you met someone?"

"Yeah. And you know, I thought I'd got past the whole 'not wanting a relationship' thing because she's different."

"What happened?"

"She's convinced that we're too different. And she needs guarantees."

His mother nodded. "Except there are no guarantees. You just…take your chances and hope."

"I've been scared to hope," he admitted.

"Me, too," she replied, and in an odd move, she reached over and touched his hand. "But Cole, I fell in love with Edward all those years ago. It didn't end well, and my heart was quite broken, but we've got a second chance. And that's really quite lovely. Maybe you and this woman—"

"Brooklyn," he supplied.

"Brooklyn. Maybe you can work things out. Because I do want you to be happy, Cole. Don't wait to be my age to share your heart with someone."

His throat tightened and he swallowed. "Well. I think this is the deepest conversation we've ever had."

"And long overdue." She smiled again and reached for her coffee.

"I'm happy for you," he said, meaning it wholeheartedly. "And I know you probably are planning some elaborate trip for your honeymoon, but you and Edward are welcome to stay on the island if you want. I have a couple who are working as caretaker and housekeeper there, and all it'll take is me sending word and they can have things readied for you."

"Does this mean you'll come to the wedding?" she asked, leaning forward, her voice hopeful. "Because I thought you'd be angry with me for marrying again."

He shook his head. "Dad's gone. Why would I want you to be alone and lonely? If you're happy, then I'm happy for you. Simple as that."

Tears filled her eyes. "We were such cold parents. I don't know where you got your big heart."

"Not everyone sees it," he assured her, chuckling. "Just a select few."

"Like this Brooklyn woman?"

He shook his head again. "Maybe before, but not now. She kind of handed it back to me."

"Then she's a fool."

"Maybe. Maybe not. She was pretty clear that we're over."

"I'm sorry, Cole."

"Me, too." He clapped his hands together and stood. "Let's change the subject. Clearly, this is an event that calls for more than coffee. I think you should call Edward, and we can set up a lunch date and all go out together. Have some champagne. What do you say?"

She stood, as well, her face beaming with approval. "Oh, that would be lovely. I'll call your assistant so she can coordinate it with your calendar."

That one line told him everything he needed to know about his mother's relationship with his father, and with him, thus far. He shook his head. "No, Mom. You call me. You don't have to have a relationship with my assistant. You're my mother."

"You're a better son than I deserve, but I'm not going to say no. Thank you, darling. I'll call you in a few days."

She moved forward, as if to buss his cheek, but she hugged him, too, an awkward thing but welcome just the same. "Thank you," she whispered and stepped back. "And don't give up if you love her, Cole. It's a rare thing. At least try to talk to her again, and listen to what she has to say."

He walked her to the door and said goodbye. And then went back to the sofa and sat down. He put his head into his hands and sighed. He missed Brooklyn. He loved her. And he wasn't sure how to go about fighting for her. How could he leave Abbott behind forever? It was a huge responsibility, but one he wanted. It motivated him to get up in the morning, gave him a purpose. He'd be on the island for a month and then be bored out of his mind and miserable. His mother had just shown him what happened to a person who was miserable in their life.

And yet living without Brooklyn was a painful thought. And he could see no way to do both. Brooklyn had been very clear about her needs, and he also didn't want to be the reason she ventured into a life she didn't want and was unhappy.

Maybe she was right. Maybe they were from two different worlds that couldn't be reconciled.

But damn, it hurt.

CHAPTER FOURTEEN

BROOKLYN LET MARVIN off his leash and watched as he ran down the beach, spinning up sand, as if his whole ordeal had never happened. She'd been a diligent nursemaid to him, checking his incision, keeping his activity low, cooking him fresh chicken and rice until his stomach had healed. It had almost kept her mind off Cole.

Almost, but not quite.

The words he'd said to her that day still echoed in her head and made her question everything. Was she avoiding life? Hiding away on the island because it was safe and secure? Was she afraid to take a chance on them because she couldn't control the situation or the outcome?

Control. That was what it all came down to. To her, control equaled safety. Because for a very few moments one spring day, she'd had absolutely no control and she'd been in horrible danger. She didn't have to be a rocket scientist to figure that out. Her mind skittered back to the night they'd spent at the Sandpiper. He'd known, even then, hadn't he? Because he'd told her that she was in control of what happened between them. And she'd been the one to take the lead.

She and Marvin were nearly at the end of the beach when she saw two people heading down over the bluff. Dan and Raelynn, holding hands, and her heart warmed at the sight of them. It was a little bittersweet, watching their happiness. One night not long ago, she and Cole had walked down the same dune, hand in hand in the moonlight.

Marvin ran up to the couple, begging for pats as was his usual style. Moments later Brooklyn caught up to everyone. She hadn't spoken to them since Cole left. Dan had taken Cole to the mainland in the boat, and Raelynn had gone along to do some grocery shopping. They'd stopped at the house to see if Brooklyn needed anything, a truly neighborly gesture. She'd awkwardly declined.

Raelynn gave her a hug. "Oh, it's good to see you. And Marvin. He looks fully recovered."

"He is," Brooklyn answered, trying not to think of how nice that hug had felt. "And it's good to see you, too."

"Maybe now we've broken the ice and you can stop avoiding us," Raelynn continued, while Dan added a shocked, "Rae!"

"No, she's right," Brooklyn said, shaking her head. "I have been. Things ended on a weird note with Cole, and I wasn't sure what to say."

"Cole wasn't himself, either. He stomped around for the few days before he left. Wasn't fit to be around, really."

"I'm sorry."

"Not your fault," Raelynn said.

"Except maybe it is." Brooklyn watched Marvin as he raced around the dune below. "I didn't give him the answer he wanted."

"Yeah, well, he's still responsible for his reaction. So there."

"Rae…" Dan's voice held a weary caution that Brooklyn found funny. It was so very… couple-ish. Clearly they'd already had this conversation.

Marvin brought back a piece of driftwood and Dan said, "That's my cue." He took the stick and went down to the beach to play some fetch.

Raelynn watched him go. "He's mad at you for breaking Cole's heart."

Brooklyn gaped at her. "Breaking his heart? I don't think I'm capable of that."

"Oh, I think you are." Raelynn's eyebrows

shot up as she spoke. "He'd really fallen for you." Brooklyn opened her mouth to protest but Raelynn held up a hand. "I'm not saying you're wrong. I'm just saying that was the result."

Brooklyn didn't know what to say. She finally sighed and said, "We're too different. It would never work."

"Really, too different? I can't see how."

Brooklyn made a sound that was half scoff, half disbelief. "Come on, Raelynn. Look at his life, look at mine. He's a freaking billionaire, and I'm…well, I'm a thousandaire. That's about the size of my savings account."

Raelynn laughed. "Oh, for Pete's sake. That's just money. That's all…window dressing. It's in here that counts." She pressed a hand to her chest. "I've known Cole a while now. I've never seen him light up like he did with you. Or laugh. Maybe he needs someone like you. You ground him in a way bank accounts and employees never can, Brooklyn. And you need him, too."

"I do?"

Raelynn met her gaze evenly. "You're hiding away here. He can pull you out of that fear and uncertainty. And why shouldn't you enjoy some of the finer things?" She raised an eyebrow. "It won't change you, if that's what you're worried about. You're too stubborn."

Brooklyn choked on a laugh, but she kept thinking of what Raelynn had said about Cole lighting up. She'd lit up too, every time he'd walked into a room or into her front yard.

"Cole is not stuck up. If anything, he's crying out for love. He didn't have much as a kid, as far as I can tell. He's had a lot of advantages, but not that. And yet he's one of the most giving people I know, expecting nothing in return."

Brooklyn knew well enough. She'd tried to wire the money for the hotel and vet bill to him, but he'd refused the transfer. She'd thought it was because he was still angry with her. But now she wondered if it was more than that.

"I hurt him, but I didn't mean to."

"We know that. Despite Dan's attitude, we both know that. But we also think you've made a big mistake, turning him away when you could take a chance on him. On you as a couple."

Silence fell for a few minutes. They listened to the crash of the waves, and the wind, and the plaintive wail of the gulls soaring overhead. It was cold, and Brooklyn shoved her hands into her jacket pockets before her fingers turned numb.

"I'm afraid," she finally said.

"We're all afraid of something," Raelynn

answered, her voice steady and sure. "Every damned one of us. We can either let our fear rule us, or we can reach out for what we want and deserve in spite of it. Something made you quit, Brooklyn. Something made you wrap yourself in what was comforting and familiar. And that's okay for a while, but don't you want more? Don't you want love and excitement of the best kind, and surprises and…and life?"

Tears pricked the back of Brooklyn's eyes. It was basically what Cole had said to her, but without the blaze of hurt and rejection behind it. That she was avoiding life and playing it safe, and giving up the opportunity for something wonderful.

Because in all her life, there'd never been anything as wonderful as being in Cole's arms.

Could she do it? Could she go to him and ask for another chance? Could she handle a place as big and chaotic as New York, when even now she found going into unfamiliar places difficult? She wanted to believe she could, but even now, panic threaded through her, cold and tight.

"I can't leave Marvin," she said.

"Oh, good heavens. You don't even sound convincing saying that." She pointed at Dan, who was tugging on the stick that was in Marvin's mouth. "We'll take care of him. We're staying for at least another month."

Brooklyn's heart started to pound as she actually considered going to New York, fighting her demons along the way. "I don't know if my passport is still valid."

"Well, that might be a barrier. You should probably check." Raelynn was smiling now, her eyes glowing. "And we'll watch the house for you, too. Whatever you need."

"Raelynn... I don't know what to say. I'm still terrified. But I think I need to at least try, you know?" She swallowed against a lump in her throat. "I've been miserable since he left."

"He's a good man. And he loves you. Nothing in life is guaranteed, but please don't miss out on what could be wonderful because you're afraid to take a chance." Raelynn nodded toward Dan. "Trust me, the rewards can be more than you ever dreamed."

Someday, Brooklyn wanted to hear the story of Raelynn and Dan, but right now, she had some arrangements to make. She reached out and put her hand on Raelynn's forearm. "Can you help me with the details? I don't even know where to find him."

Now Raelynn's grin was wide. "Oh, yes. You find your passport. Then come up to the house and we'll get everything arranged. I'll help."

Brooklyn called for Marvin and then looked at Raelynn as a fizz of excitement started to run through her veins. "Why are you so determined to set us up?"

"Oh, honey. Because Cole is a great boss, but the few days before he left? I don't want to be stuck with that guy as my employer. He needs some Brooklyn sunshine in his life, stat."

Brooklyn grinned, then hooked Marvin up to his leash once he knocked up against her knees, tongue out and happy. "Thank you, Raelynn. I'll come back to the house when I've found my passport."

Dan came up the dune behind Marvin. "All good?" he asked.

"Better than good." Raelynn went to him and tilted her head up for a kiss. "We're going to dog-sit."

It had been years since Brooklyn had been on an airplane, and she'd found her passport though there was only six months left on it. Now she was buckled into her seat, preparing for landing at Newark airport.

The flight had been full, and since being trapped with no way out was one of the things that ramped up her anxiety, she'd spent most of the flight listening to a calming meditation app. It had helped.

With a couple of light bumps, they were on the ground, and before she knew it she'd grabbed her carry-on bag and was following the signs for ground transportation. She could do this. She could not hide forever, and this was a normal thing for most people.

It was better in the cab. The crush of people was held at bay and once she gave the driver the address, she sat back and watched the scenery as they left New Jersey for Manhattan. By ten thirty, she was dropped off outside a massive skyscraper. Inside were the executive offices of Abbott Industries, and Cole was in there, too. He didn't know she was coming. She'd thought about calling him, but then didn't want to in case she couldn't go through with it. Or... for him to tell her not to. She shouldered her bag, straightened the thick wrap she wore, and made her way inside.

One step closer.

Up the elevator, ten, twenty, twenty-five floors...

The doors opened and she thought she might be sick. Instead, she took a deep inhale and stepped off the elevator. She'd tackled some big things. She'd got on a plane and come here, faced crowds and a bit of the unknown and all because Cole Abbott might just be in love with her...and it was time she started living her life instead of settling for half of one. It had taken Cole to shake her out of that, so why would she let him slip away without fighting for him?

"May I help you?" The receptionist's voice was warm and pleasant, and Brooklyn stepped forward.

"Oh, yes, I'm sorry. I'm here to see Cole Abbott."

"Do you have an appointment?"

"No, I'm afraid I don't." Oh, Lord, what if he wasn't in the office today? Or stuck in meetings?

"He's in a meeting at the moment, but I can let him know you're here. It might be a bit of a wait, I'm sorry."

"I don't mind."

"Your name, please?"

More misgivings. What if this woman said her name and he didn't come out? "Brooklyn Graves," she answered, that sick feeling overtaking her again. What was she even doing here?

Then she straightened her shoulders and lifted her chin. She was here because for the first time in the past several years, something was more important to her than protecting herself. It was time she listened to her heart. And her heart said that there was something between her and Cole that was special, and that she'd been a fool to send him away as she had.

She kept going back to what Raelynn had said—that deep down they were the same sort of person, and the rest was just trappings. God, she hoped so.

So she waited in the seating area, dressed in a hand-knit shawl and clutching her ancient carry-on bag, daring to hope.

She didn't have long to wait. Cole came rushing around the corner, his tie slightly askew, his hair ruffled. His gaze clashed with hers and he stopped abruptly and stared.

"It is you. I couldn't believe it when I got the message."

Brooklyn was light-headed and her knees shook as she stood. "She said you were in a meeting. I didn't want to interrupt. I can wait…"

He shook his head. "No, the meeting can wait. We'll break until this afternoon. Come with me so we can talk."

She followed him down the hall to an office that was as big as her living room and kitchen combined. There was a massive desk on one side of the space, so neat and tidy she wondered if it was just for show. There was also a credenza and a five-foot filing cabinet, all in the same rich wood. In front of the desk was a smaller table with four chairs around it, as if for a small working group.

The other side of the office was made for

comfort. There was a sofa, a couple of chairs, a beautiful glass-topped table; a couple of tall plants added some warmth to the space, and there was artwork on the walls. Best of all was the view of the river. She went to the window and stared out. This was such a different world from her own, but she found herself intrigued nonetheless.

"Surprised?" he asked.

"No." She turned and offered a small smile. "But then, I have no frame of reference, really. Other than, I don't know, movies."

He chuckled, and his eyes softened. "God, it's good to see you." Her throat tightened, and she was about to respond when he added, "What are you doing here?"

This was the moment to be brave, wasn't it? She'd come all this way, stepped out of her comfort zone, to be able to say the words she'd rehearsed. And now they were all gone.

His smile faded. "Is there something wrong? Did something happen?"

"Oh, no! Nothing like that. I'm just...now that I'm here I'm not sure how..." She sighed, met his gaze. "You were right, Cole, and I was wrong."

Lines furrowed his brow. "Wrong about what?"

She took a step forward, her pulse hammering with nerves, her breath short but feeling like she was on a train picking up speed, and no choice but to just go where it led. "About us. About me. You offered me something that I didn't know how to accept. That I was afraid to accept, because it meant leaving my comfortable, safe life behind." She ran her fingers through her hair. "Oh, Lord. What was I gonna do? Stay on that island forever, so I never had to put myself out there? How ridiculous."

He took two strides and took her by the hands. "Not ridiculous. You went through something life-altering, and you sought out comfort. How can I judge you for that when I did the same thing?"

"You did?"

"Sure. What did I do after my dad died? I buried myself in work until I couldn't hide from things anymore. And I thought I'd come a long way, but then there was you. I've never met anyone like you, Brooklyn. And yeah, maybe you were playing it safe, but you also know how to find joy in small things, to appreciate the simple, to value what money can't buy. You were so good for me, how could I not fall for you?"

The anxiety fluttered away, but her pulse was still racing, this time with hope and anticipation. "Raelynn said that we are similar underneath the obvious differences. I still don't know how to exist in your world. Maybe I'll never fit in. But Cole, I want to try. You changed everything this fall. Ever since the robbery, I've merely existed. But with you, I felt so alive. So I'm here to say that if you still want to give us a chance, I'm in. You might have to be patient with me, is all."

His smile grew until he was practically beaming. "You mean that."

"I got on a plane and braved the big city to find you. Would I have done that if I didn't mean it?"

"I'm sorry that you're still afraid—"

She waved him off. "No, don't be. The truth is, I'm still afraid because I've never made myself face it. I couldn't face so many things. I alienated people. I don't speak to my siblings enough, or my parents. I hide out on the island saying it's all nostalgia but it's not. Don't get me wrong, I love what I do. But that's not the same thing, is it?"

He shook his head. "It's not. I love what I do, too. But it's a lonely thing going it alone. And any time I was with you, everything was brighter. I wasn't lying, Brooklyn. I fell in love with you."

"I fell in love with you, too. I was just doing

what I always do—be scared. I think I'd like to try something different now."

He wrapped his arms around her and held her close. "That's such good news," he whispered, kissing her hair by her temple. "Oh, Brooklyn, I've really missed you these past few weeks."

"Me, too. I moped around all the time. Tried convincing myself that I'd been right, sending you away. I'm going to be honest. It didn't take much convincing on Raelynn's part. She played matchmaker, but I didn't make it very hard for her."

"Remind me to give her a raise," he said, hugging her tightly.

"She and Dan are keeping Marvin while I'm here," she replied. "You blew into my life with your big real estate offer, but I ended up with two new friends, too."

Cole leaned back a little and looked into her eyes, then kissed her. A "Welcome home" kiss, a "Thank God you're here" kiss, an "I love you" kiss. Nothing had ever felt so good, so beautiful, so very right.

And when he let her go, she put her hands on either side of his face and smiled at him, tears gathering at the corners of her eyes. "I want to stop being afraid. I want to make you proud and fit in, but I don't want to lose myself. You can understand that, right?"

"Of course I can." He put one of his hands over hers. "I'll tell you something Jeremy and Bran don't know. When I had my breakdown, I started seeing a therapist to help me navigate my way out of the darkness. If you're willing, we can get you some help, too. Your fears are real, sweetheart. But you don't have to figure it out alone."

She nodded, so very, very touched, particularly that he'd made himself vulnerable, too. "I did some counseling after the robbery, and it helped, but it wasn't enough. I've always known that, deep down."

"Then I'll support you with whatever you need." He squeezed her fingers. "And that is not contingent on us being together, okay?"

He was such a good person. To think she'd thought him an arrogant billionaire flaunting about in his helicopter. He was so, so much more.

Then he kissed her again. "To be honest, if you hadn't shown up here, I was going to head back to the island soon. I know I left in a huff. I wanted to try again, to talk, to see if we could find a way through it. But I'm not complaining that you beat me to it."

He smiled again, then led her to the sofa and

they sat. "I think if you're up to it, you should have a nice visit here for a week or two, and then go back to the island. You'll be missing Marvin, I'm sure. And I'll be joining you a week or so after that."

"You will?" She was thrilled.

"My mother is getting married, and I've convinced her to spend a few days with Edward at the house. That is, if you don't mind me bunking in with you."

Of course she didn't mind.

"They're honeymooning in Nova Scotia in November?" She faked a chill and laughed. "How'd that happen?"

"Oh, don't be silly. They're spending a few nights there. Then they're off to Italy for three weeks."

"And you're okay with the new man?"

Cole nodded. "I've known him my whole life. It's a long story, but it explains so much of my childhood. She came to see me, and she really talked to me for the first time. I'm starting to let go of a lot of my resentment. And it made me miss you even more. My parents didn't have warmth in their marriage, but I feel it every time we're together. We have something special, Brooklyn."

"We do," she answered. "More than I ever dreamed possible."

CHAPTER FIFTEEN

FOR THE FIRST time since the island had been settled, there was a wedding on its shores. The May sun was shining, the gulls were calling, and the waves were sending little frothy fingers over the sand as Brooklyn walked barefoot toward Cole, holding a bouquet reminiscent of wildflowers—baby pink roses, marguerites, baby's breath, purple clover. It was as wild and simple as she was, perfectly suited for an island bride on her wedding day.

He was waiting, in a suit the color of the sand beneath her feet, his brilliant blue eyes crinkling at the corners as he smiled at her walking down the "aisle." Her dress flowed softly around her curves, the silk caressing her skin as the breeze off the ocean fluttered the fabric around her legs. She'd anticipated the wind, so she'd left her hair mostly down in tumbling waves, except for a little from each side pulled back to anchor the frothy veil now billowing behind her.

For a simple look it had cost a fortune, but Cole's mother had insisted on taking her shopping in New York. She'd invited Brooklyn's mother along, as well, and while Brooklyn had been apprehensive about it, the two had gotten along just fine.

It seemed that Brooklyn sometimes erected barriers when there were none.

Now she was nearly to Cole, her heart bursting, wondering how on earth she'd got this lucky. Raelynn had preceded her up the aisle in her own dress of blush pink that matched the pale tea roses in their bouquets. Branson was Cole's best man, while Jeremy had performed usher duties and Dan was in charge of Marvin, who wore a white bow tie for the occasion.

Nearly there now, where the officiant waited. Past Jen and Delilah from the yarn store, past Branson's new wife, Jessica, who was expecting their first child, past Tori and Jeremy and her family and Cole's mother and her new husband.

And then she was there, standing beside him, reaching for his hand.

She'd moved her engagement ring to her right hand, and he toyed with it now, turning the stone in his fingers—a whopping two-carat cushion cut with a diamond-encrusted band that had nearly blinded her when he'd opened the box.

And then she met his gaze and was lost. Everything disappeared—the guests, the wind and the gulls and the ocean and there was just him, loving her, and her loving him, and the person in front of them, joining them to each other forever. Her lower lip wobbled as she said her vows; his voice was strong and clear as he made his promises. He slid a wedding band over her finger, and she did the same, pushing the platinum circle over his knuckle until it nested perfectly where it would remain. And then they kissed, and her veil whipped around her head, enveloping them in a curtain of tulle as a cheer went up from the small assembly.

Marvin barked at the commotion, and Brooklyn hadn't believed until this moment that it was possible to be this happy.

Back at the house, tents were set up and tables were covered with fine white linens and bouquets of flowers matching the one in her hand. A photographer took photos in the gardens and on the staircase in the house, and then they joined the guests who were mingling with cocktails. A delicious aroma rose from a line of chafing dishes; Cole had insisted on bringing his favorite caterer from New York to prepare the feast for the gathering, and even the cocktail hour was nothing short of amazing, with magnificent crab cakes, smoked salmon, asparagus tips wrapped in prosciutto, and a wine list that would grace the finest Michelin-starred establishment.

The dinner to follow was no less perfect, with lobster bisque, filet, and a crème wedding cake with fresh strawberry filling.

And through it all, Cole held his wife's hand as often as possible. Brooklyn had never felt so adored.

And when the evening descended, Brooklyn changed into a going-away dress. The guests would all remain on the island for the night, comfortably ensconced in the beautiful rooms of the mansion. Meanwhile, Dave and his helicopter flew in to escort them away for their wedding night. He took them back to the site of their last helicopter trip, the tiny Liverpool airport, where a chartered plane waited to take them to Martha's Vineyard. They'd spend a week there, hidden away from the world.

Brooklyn fell asleep, her head against Cole's shoulder as they made their way over the dark ocean to their honeymoon site. She woke when they landed and smiled bashfully as he kissed her hair. "Glad you had a refresher," he whispered. "Our night is just beginning."

Heat crept up her cheeks, the delicious sort.

He was right, of course. But while they'd planned their day to the last detail, she still had one surprise left. A wedding present he was not expecting.

She waited until they were in the suite. Despite the coolness of the evening, Cole had opened the door to the private balcony just a little so that the light curtains ruffled and the scent of the ocean came inside. The room was lovely, all white and china blue, an oasis of calm and relaxation where they could settle into their first married days together. Cole stripped off his tie and his suit jacket, hanging them over a chair. He looked delicious in wrinkled trousers and his white shirt open at the throat. And they'd make the most of the king-size bed, she was sure of it.

As if reading her thoughts, he crossed the room and gathered her in his arms, then kissed her, holding nothing back. When he let her go, she was rather dizzy from it all, and looking forward to the rest of the night. But she put a palm on his chest and willed herself to calm.

"Wait," she said softly. "I have a wedding gift for you, and I've been waiting all day to give it to you when we were alone."

"Oh?" He waggled his eyebrows. "Tell me it's some skimpy lingerie under that dress."

She laughed. "That, too. But this is something else. Something special." She reached into the pocket of her new carry-on bag and took out a thick envelope.

"What's this?"

"Open it and find out."

He sat down on the edge of the bed and slid open the seal. Brooklyn watched as what the papers represented registered, and his gaze darted up to hers. "This is the deed to the house and your land."

"Now it's our house and our land. All you have to do is sign."

He stared at the sheaf of papers again, as if he couldn't quite believe it. "But Brooklyn, that's yours. It's been in your family for generations."

Oh, the dear man. She went to him and sat beside him on the mattress, and put her hand on his knee. "You silly fool. After today, you're my family. Now the whole island is back where it belongs. With one owner, one who loves and cherishes it."

For the past six months she'd discovered the true depths of her love for Cole. There had been moments where she wasn't sure she could handle city life and the demands that went along with his status, but she'd adjusted. She'd started going to therapy again, too, rather than hiding away and denying her fears. But the island was still their place, where they'd met and fallen in love and the place they loved most of all. It would be a summer home for them, a vacation house and a refuge when they needed time away. And someday, their children would run along the beach and collect driftwood and they'd go out and fish for pollock and mackerel.

"Sweetheart. This is just…thank you. Thank you for trusting me with it, for sharing this with me."

"I thought we could stay in the big house and Dan and Rae could have the house if they wanted it. Like you originally planned."

"Are you sure? You have so many memories there. I remember you saying you wouldn't take two million dollars for the house and land. But here you are just…giving it to me."

"That's because I got something much more valuable than two million dollars," she whispered, snuggling close. "I got your heart. And my love, I can't put a price on that. It's worth everything."

"I love you, Mrs. Abbott." The letter dropped to the floor as he pulled her into his arms.

"And I love you, Mr. Abbott. Happy wedding day."

* * * * *

*If you missed the previous stories in the
South Shore Billionaires trilogy,
look out for*

Christmas Baby for the Billionaire
Beauty and the Brooding Billionaire

*And if you enjoyed this story,
check out these other great reads from
Donna Alward*

Summer Escape with the Tycoon
Secret Millionaire for the Surrogate
Best Man for the Wedding Planner

All available now!